LEGEND TRIP

A Dreadful Penny Novella

J. MATTHEW SAUNDERS

SAINT GEORGE'S PRESS

LEGEND TRIP
A DREADFUL PENNY NOVELLA

Cover photography copyright © kenny1 (graveyard) and
Luis Molinero (man),
courtesy of Shutterstock

Printed in the United States of America

First Printing, 2019

e-book ISBN 978-1-7329313-2-9
paperback ISBN 978-1-7329313-3-6

Saint George's Press
York, S.C.
www.saintgeorgespress.com

LEGEND TRIP

1.

DEATH IS NOT THE END the preacher tells you at the funeral. You'll see your loved one again someday, in the Sweet By-and-By. It's an easy thing for him to say. He says it a lot at a lot of funerals.

But you—you're the one who has to believe it. You're the one who has to look at the unnaturally beautiful face of your mother, or your brother, or—God forbid—your child, and have faith. And as the days wear on and as that faith begins to fade, where is he? Where is that son-of-a-bitch preacher with his empty platitudes and hollow promises?

But what if you didn't need faith? What if you had the chance to know for sure that the person you loved more than anything was okay and that someday you would see them again? How far would you go for that certainty? What would you give up?

Penelope set the rock down on her desk. She had managed to get most of the blood off. She accidentally took off some of the paint, too, but not much. She'd made the paperweight for her father when she was eight. It had a yellow and orange sun on one side and a green tree on the other. He'd used it every day until the day he died.

She stared at it hoping it would move, just a little, to prove he was still there. Ever since the night his ghost had flung it across the room to save her and her friends from Patrick Wheeler—a magician with a grudge and some heavy firepower—she hadn't had any sign of her father at all, nothing, not even the usual knocks he used to communicate with her. One for *no* and two for *yes*.

Penelope sighed. "Dad, I miss you. I wish you could talk to me. Can you hear me? Please do something to let me know you're still here."

But she was met with only silence.

Once he unlocked the door, Zed and his companion slipped quickly inside the bookstore.

"Isn't this against one of Mr. Keller's rules?" Jake Dempsey asked as Zed grabbed his hand and pulled him through the darkened maze of bookshelves.

Mr. Keller, the owner of the bookstore, posted a set of rules that included such things as no religious discussions and no excessive browsing. Everyone thought the rules were amusing, but no one dared break them when Mr. Keller was around.

"It's absolutely against one of his rules," Zed called over his shoulder, "but he's out of town, and you have to admit this is as safe a spot as we're going to find."

He'd suggested the bookstore on a whim. He didn't know exactly why, other than he wanted to talk to Jake alone, away from other people, afraid they might overhear. And he was a little drunk. Zed took a seat on the floor in the history section and leaned his back against a bookshelf.

Jake sat down next to him. "So now what?"

Zed rested his head on Jake's shoulder. He caught a whiff of the subtle cologne Jake wore. "I don't know. I hadn't thought that far."

"You're awfully comfortable with this."

"With what?"

"With this. Being close."

Zed made to move away. "Well, if it's going to be a problem for you …"

"No, not at all," Jake said hastily. "It's just that when you told me you'd dated women before, I just figured—"

"That this was just some sort of attempt to satisfy my curiosity?"

Jake shrugged. "Well, a little. Hope you're not offended."

Zed chuckled. "It's going to take more than that to offend me. I've just always been attracted to people as people. Man or woman, it's never made a difference."

Jake lowered his voice almost to a whisper. "Does your family know?"

"I don't have any family besides my mom. And she knows. I told her a long time ago."

"And she's okay with it?"

"I don't think she completely understands, but she always taught me to be myself, no matter what. What about you?"

Jake shook his head. "Oh, no. I've never told anyone. My family would never speak to me again, not that I'm really talking to them now. It might have been easier to tell them I'm a faggot than I'm volunteering for McGovern's presidential campaign."

"Sorry about that."

Jake sighed. "It's hard when you don't know who to trust.

One careless move and you're out of a job, or worse. Although, I guess I don't have to worry about the job thing right now, not like you. You have to worry about three."

Zed kept quiet about his relationships at work. Jake was right. He'd be fired in a heartbeat from the radio station, and Mr. Keller had no trouble making his opinions on the matter known. But Penelope, that was different. He considered her a friend. He didn't think she'd really care who he dated, but even so, he'd never told her. He could try to convince himself the topic had just never come up, but that would be a lie.

He grasped Jake's hand. "I guess it's good to find people we can trust, right?"

Maybe the few beers he'd had were giving Zed some fortitude, or maybe it was because he could sense Jake's anticipation, but either way, Zed leaned over and kissed him. Jake returned the favor while running his fingers through Zed's hair.

Then suddenly Jake's body went limp.

"Jake?"

Zed didn't have time to say anything more than that, though, because a bolt of lightning ran through his body. A flash of white light blinded him, and when his sight cleared, he wasn't in the bookstore anymore. Just like the last time he and Jake shared a vision, he found himself alone in the forest on a chilly night. Pale moonlight filtered down through the canopy. Stepping over tree roots and pushing back branches, he moved through the woods with a purpose, though he didn't know what that purpose was. He hadn't noticed before the palmetto trees among the oaks and pines and beech trees. He must have been somewhere in the Low Country.

A howl rose up that sent a chill down his spine. He had heard that sound before. Shadows rolled and rippled at the edges of his vision. He picked up his pace, but the shadows followed. They grew and multiplied, taking on form—long, loping limbs and heads with canine snouts and glowing green eyes—daemons—just like the ones Patrick Wheeler compelled into his service, but he and Charles and Penelope had stopped Patrick Wheeler, hadn't they? Suddenly, the shadows surged toward him, and he took off running through the woods.

Branches scraped his hands and face. He stumbled more than once, but he didn't dare stop. He knew what those things could do. They called to him in his head, telling him awful things, trying to make him despair and lose hope. He focused on putting one foot in front of the other, but even he couldn't run forever. Eventually he'd get tired, and the things would get him.

He stumbled over what he thought was just another rock, but it had a flat face and sharp edges—a gravestone. He'd found the graveyard from the first vision. He struggled to his feet, but it was too late. The shadows overtook him.

And then Zed was back in the bookstore, lying on the floor, staring up at the ceiling. He pushed himself up. Jake lay next to him. He didn't move when Zed nudged him. Zed felt for a pulse and found a thready one. He shook Jake a little harder, calling his name and working what little magic he could to get Jake to wake up. When that didn't work, he looked around frantically, trying to figure out what to do. He'd carry Jake to the hospital if he had to.

"Happiness," Jake croaked.

Zed knelt down over him. "Jake?"

The other man opened his eyes and sat up slowly. "Man, what…"

Jake met Zed's gaze. Fear came off him in waves. He scrambled to his feet.

Zed grabbed his arm. "Wait. Don't run this time, please.

Can't we just talk?"

"There were … things in the woods, with green eyes," Jake said.

Zed nodded. "I know."

"And you knew what they were."

"Yes, I did."

Jake was silent for a moment. When he spoke, his words had a hard edge. "I was honest with you. I think the least you can do is be honest with me."

Zed nodded. "You're right. I'm sorry. My detective work is a little more interesting than I let on."

Morning sunlight streamed into Charles' bedroom. When he pushed back the covers and sat up in bed, he shivered. It had gotten chilly overnight, the first really cold night in a long time. He crossed bare wood floor to close his bedroom window.

The scene outside the window was a busy street in Harlem in 1919, far from Greenville, South Carolina, in 1972. Here he was Isaiah Jenkins, a former World War I soldier and now the manager of a jazz spot called the Blue Club.

And he had a breakfast date.

Half an hour later, freshly showered and dressed, Charles stepped outside into the crisp air. Everyone he passed wore coats and scarves not seen since April. The leaves on the trees in the park were edged in orange and yellow and red.

He saw her before she saw him. Wearing a dark red dress with a fur coat and stole, she sat at a table at a sidewalk café while sipping a cup of coffee and nibbling on a pastry. Not only was she beautiful, but Millie Priest had the most remarkable voice Charles had ever heard. She was whip-smart, too. Millie had always managed her own career. She knew how to pack a house and make sure she got her cut of the take.

When their eyes met, he smiled and waved. She smiled back, and his heart skipped a beat. He slipped into the seat opposite her. They talked about easy things for a little while. Charles drank his coffee and watched people go by. Isaiah's memories were all there, right next to his own. As they chatted, it was easy for him to think of himself as Isaiah.

Charles was the bad dream.

"I was thinking about wearing the dark blue dress tonight," she said after taking a sip of her coffee, "the one with the white rose on the sleeve. What do you think?"

"You know that's one of my favorites. You trying to distract me from my job? Hard enough as it is when you're up there."

She smiled, but it seemed strained somehow. "There's going to be some important people in the audience tonight. We need to impress them."

Charles frowned. "Important people? Who are you talking about?"

She hesitated. "You know how the Blue Club has had a couple of lean months."

"Yeah, but they've been just that. Lean months. We'll bounce back."

"Lewis isn't so sure." She glanced down at her half-eaten Danish and lowered her voice. "He's worried about what happens when we can't serve booze anymore."

Lewis was the owner of the Blue Club, and he wasn't wrong to be worried. Charles, too, wondered what would happen when Prohibition stopped the liquor from flowing.

Charles leaned forward and waited until Millie met his gaze again. "You know the drinks aren't what brings people out. It's you they're coming to see."

"Some people are thinking about investing. That's all."

Charles leaned back again. "Who?"

She shook her head. "I don't know their names. Only Lewis does."

"How come you know before I do? I'm supposed to be the manager."

"He pulled me aside last night, told me to pick out my best dress and my best songs."

Charles' ire rose. "He should tell me himself rather than leave it up to you to do it."

"I'm sure he'll talk to you tonight."

"He'd better, or there's going to be hell to pay."

She placed a hand on his and made him unball his fist. "Isaiah, behave now. All you have to do is make sure everything runs smoothly, just like you always do, okay?" Her smile returned. "Stop by the dressing room tonight after the set when you get a chance. I have a present for you."

"A present? What is it?"

She laughed. "It's a surprise."

The tension in his shoulders eased somewhat. "What if I don't want to wait?"

She stood, but her hand lingered. "Just be patient. I promise you'll like it."

He watched her walk away and vanish into the throng of people.

That evening, as he always did, Charles oversaw the last-minute touches before the patrons were let into the Blue Club—making sure the tablecloths were straight, the silverware polished, and the glasses clean—but he couldn't shake the nagging worry at the back of his mind.

The worry eased somewhat as the club filled up. Everything ran smoothly at first. The Bill Porter Three—piano, bass, and trumpet—played their low-key set as everyone drank their cocktails, but about ten minutes before Millie was supposed to go on stage, a small commotion erupted at the door. A group of people entered the club, a dark-skinned man dressed in a midnight blue three-piece suit leading the way. Even the Blue Club bouncers gave the heavies on either side of him a wide berth.

A ripple of murmurs ran through the crowd. The man was Andre Lestrade, who styled himself a businessman. Charles had learned about him while working at the docks. Nothing went on in Harlem without Andre having a finger in it, legal or not.

What's he doing here?

He can't be the investor Millie was talking about, not him.

Charles knew better than to tell him he wasn't welcome at the Blue Club, but the least he could do was make sure Andre understood trouble wouldn't be tolerated. Before he could get to Andre, though, Lewis intercepted the businessman, an ear-to-ear grin on his face. The club owner took Andre's hand and shook it enthusiastically, then led him and his entourage to a group of tables near the stage. Several waiters came over immediately.

For the moment, Charles retreated. He'd have a talk with Lewis later. No good could come from throwing in with a man like Andre Lestrade.

The lights dimmed, and Millie came on stage, dazzling as always. This was Charles' favorite part of the day, but he couldn't enjoy her set. He kept glancing at Andre and his entourage. Millie, too, looked Andre's way more than once. Usually Charles could imagine she was singing only to him, but that night it was obvious she was singing to someone else.

To make matters worse, after Millie's set was over, she didn't retreat backstage like she normally did. She went over to Andre's table and sat in the chair next to him, recently vacated by one of his bodyguards. Charles watched as Andre crept closer, putting his arm on the back of her chair, placing a hand on top of hers. She smiled and laughed occasionally as the Bill Porter Three played their second set. Eventually, she stood and took her leave, but not before accepting a kiss on the hand from Andre.

In the small hours of the morning, after the club closed and all the patrons had gone home, Charles went to Millie's dressing room. He knocked three times like he always did.

"Come in," a muffled voice called from inside.

Charles opened the door. Millie sat at her dressing table.

Her smile faded as soon as she saw the expression on his face. "What's wrong?"

"What's wrong? Do you know who was at the club tonight? That was Andre Lestrade."

"I know who he is." Her expression became a little more guarded.

"Why was he here?"

"I think you can figure out why."

"Why didn't you tell me before?"

She gestured at him. "Because of this. Because of how you're acting now."

"But he's dangerous," Charles said. "We can't take money from him."

"We have to do something."

Charles shook his head. "No. There's got to be another way."

"Trust me, Isaiah. If Lewis thought there was another way, he would do it. We can't lose the Blue Club."

Charles took a deep breath. "You let him put his arm

around you."

"Yes, I *let* him." She squared her jaw. "And that's all I let him do."

"What if he wants to do more next time?" Charles asked.

Unbidden, the image of Millie in her blue sequined dress stained with blood came to his mind. Her ghost had revealed to him that she died on March 18, 1920, in the real world, less than six months away. He'd spent a lot of time thinking about how he could stop her death.

"There's not going to be a next time," she replied. "He was just coming over tonight to check out the place and talk to Lewis."

"And if he invests? Don't you think he'll be here a lot more?"

She glared. "What kind of girl do you take me for, Isaiah Jenkins? I am a singer. I am a professional."

"I'm not talking about you. I just know that sometimes men in his position don't take no for an answer."

"Well, he will take it from me."

Charles wiped a hand across his face. "Millie, this is a bad idea."

"It's not your decision to make, Isaiah."

"I just worry."

"Too much." She stood and came across the room and placed a hand on his chest. "Nothing is ever going to separate us. Do you understand?"

He covered her hand with his. "I want to believe that."

"Then believe."

He leaned down and kissed her. She melted into his embrace.

Charles woke up in his own bed in his own house, surrounded by his books. The moonlight shown through the curtains that moved like ghosts in the breeze. He sat up, buried his face in his hands, and sobbed.

Ephraim Brown turned on the television and fell into the recliner. His clothes still held the faint whiff of the blackberry root he'd burned as part of the ritual, but at the moment, he didn't care. He was tired. Louise was still in Virginia, and Bertram was on a camping trip somewhere in North Carolina, so no one was there to question him about it. He'd take a shower later.

The news was full of reports that a truce had been reached in the fighting between North and South Vietnam. At least they weren't talking about the break-in at the Watergate Hotel anymore. He was sick of hearing about that, just the news making a big deal out of nothing. There was also a small update about the murder of the Israeli athletes at the Munich Olympics. Everyone always acted shocked when such evil things happened, but Ephraim knew you only had to look at your own back yard to find evil—just look at his.

His company destroyed, his family attacked, his employees murdered. The police hadn't caught the murderer, but Bertram told him the person who did it had been taken care of. Bertram didn't offer any more than that, and Ephraim didn't ask any questions. But now it was time to take charge of things again. He was going to make sure no one could harm his family any more.

Ephraim awoke to the test pattern on the television screen. He must have dozed off. He stood and turned off the television, figuring he ought to get things cleaned up. Bertram was supposed to come home the next day, and he didn't want to have to answer any awkward questions. Some small part of him had hoped to reconnect with his son after he moved back to Greenville, but those hopes had been dashed also. Everything would be sorted out soon, though, he told himself. He just needed a little more time, and he'd get his family back. He'd get everything back.

The back door opened and closed. Bertram coming home early, Ephraim's groggy brain told him, though that didn't exactly make sense. He expected to hear footsteps on the stairs or the clatter of cabinets from the kitchen as his son rummaged for something to eat, but there was only silence. Ephraim glanced over his shoulder. The silhouette of a figure stood in the doorway.

"Bertram? Is that you?" he called out.

The figure entered the room without taking a step. In a blink, it simply stood a few feet closer. Ephraim grasped the charm he wore around his neck. It didn't do any good. Another blink, and the dark thing was on top of him, two green glowing dots where its eyes should have been.

"No, not—"

Ephraim never got a chance to finish the sentence before he was lost to the darkness.

Bertram eyed the cute blonde at the other end of the bar. Their gazes met briefly before she smiled, tucked a piece of stray hair behind her ear, and turned away. Any other night he would have ambled over and introduced himself, but not that night.

He slid his empty glass over and flagged down the bartender for another beer. He came into the bar just off the highway near Asheville intending to muster up some courage to go home. Otherwise he didn't know if he'd have the guts to talk to his dad the next day and tell him he was leaving.

He didn't have any reason to stay in Greenville. Not anymore. He'd come back to help his dad run the company, but the warehouse for the Brown Tractor & Farm Supply Co. was destroyed in a freak explosion, one helped along by a demon-possessed tractor. There was no company to run. He'd tried to help pick up the pieces, but lately his dad seemed to want to take care of things himself.

He didn't like how secretive his dad was being. Something strange was going on, and given everything he had learned over the last several months, Bertram knew strange. But he couldn't stay. He'd never had a better chance to figure out what he wanted for his own life, away from the family business. He hadn't worked out exactly where he'd go. Maybe back to Atlanta. Or Knoxville even. He had some buddies up there. Someone had to know about a job he could take.

When he looked up again, the blonde was gone. A scan of the room revealed her near the door on the arm of another guy. Just as well. He wasn't really in the mood, because there was one other reason he didn't want to stay in town.

Her name was Penelope.

He still cringed every time he thought of the words Patrick Wheeler had said when he was wearing Bertram's face, when he was holding Bertram at knife-point, ready to sacrifice him for whatever ritual he planned. About how he'd basically thrown himself at Penelope when they were teenagers. About how he wanted to be more than friends. About how she'd never noticed. It was all true. Everything he'd said was true, but Bertram had never told anyone else how he felt. How did Patrick Wheeler know?

He just wanted to get as far away from magic as he could. As he stared at the bottom of yet another empty glass, he wished he'd never come back.

2.

Tuesday, October 24, 1972

PENELOPE PULLED HER BLACK LINCOLN onto Church Street. In front of her, the city spread out, brown and gray against the bright blue sky. She could count about a half dozen church steeples reaching heavenward. She wondered how many people knew there was a whole other world underneath the one they saw.

Of course, her pastor would say that there were other realms of existence. Heaven and Hell were real places. Angels and demons were real beings, fighting every day over people's souls. She'd never met any angels, though, only demons, and it seemed like she and her friends were the only ones fighting against them. Her father had fought too, until he was shot and killed in a botched robbery. She missed him. She really could have talked with him right then.

When Penelope stepped into the Grayson & Sons antique shop, she nearly turned around to see if she'd accidentally walked into the wrong shop. She expected the usual tidal wave of furniture, paintings, lamps, china, and a thousand kinds of knick-knacks. But that day, she found everything meticulously arranged in perfect vignettes, as all the things might look in a real home. In fact, Penelope was reminded a little too much of all her older relatives' houses. There was an unwritten list of acceptable furnishings for a Southern home of a certain stature, and Dan Kowalczyk, owner of the shop, had everything on that list in spades.

Dan came from somewhere in the back of the store. When he saw her, his face broke out in a wide smile. "Penelope. How are you?"

"Great, Dan. And you?" She continued to gape at all the neatly arranged antiques.

He followed her gaze. "It's a big change I know. Do you like it?"

"It's certainly different."

"It was Barbara's idea. She said it might help people to envision things in their own homes if we arranged the inventory in a more natural way."

Barbara was Dan's new assistant. His former assistant, Mary, was murdered by the magician Roy Arnold. The part Penelope never told Dan was that a demon Roy Arnold controlled actually committed the deed.

Penelope frowned. "It just seems so … orderly. Don't you think it takes away some of the sense of adventure?"

Dan shrugged. "Maybe, but it also increased sales by fifteen percent. Barbara was definitely onto something."

Barbara, in addition to being friendly and attractive, was frighteningly competent, and she annoyed Penelope.

"Is she here?" Penelope asked.

He shook his head. "Not today. It's her day off. What brings you by? Better circumstances than the last time I hope."

The last time Penelope had visited Dan, she had just been rear-ended by someone driving a gold Ford, the first of a few threatening incidents, including a brick thrown through her office window. Nothing new had happened for a couple of months, though, and Penelope hoped whoever it was had gotten it out of their system.

"Thankfully, yes. I have a question for you."

"Sure. Ask away."

Penelope opened her purse and pulled out an envelope. Inside was a silver locket in the shape of a heart. "I have a friend whose grandmother just passed away. She found this locket and wanted to know if it was valuable."

Dan grinned. "Back to the dead grandmother line?"

The first time they met, Penelope had tried to get information out of him by making up a story about her recently departed grandmother. To her dismay, he saw right through that lie.

"It's true this time," she lied.

The locket came from her friend Carolyn Cole, who worked at the Division of Public Records. A secret admirer left it at her door. She gave it to Penelope so Penelope could try to figure out who had given it to her.

Dan smirked as he held out his hand. "May I?"

She handed over the locket.

He squinted and held it up to the light. "Does your 'friend' know anything about it at all?"

Penelope pretended she didn't notice the stress on the word *friend*. "Not really. She never saw her grandmother wearing it. She told me she just found it in the back of a drawer."

That last lie she was particularly proud of.

Dan opened the locket and examined the inside. "Wow, it's a shame it stayed hidden."

"What do you mean?"

He leaned forward and pointed to the inside surface of

the locket. "See these markings here? That's the hallmark of the silversmith. This locket was made by a Swedish silversmith named Lars Dahlberg around 1870."

"So, it's over a hundred years old."

He nodded. "I'd say it's probably worth about twenty dollars, even with the broken clasp. Not a huge amount, but nothing to sneeze at either. That's what your friend wanted to know, right?"

Not exactly.

Penelope tried not to let her disappointment show. "I think she was hoping for more of a story. This Lars Dahlberg, are a lot of pieces by him still around? How likely would someone here have something by him?"

Dan shrugged. "I don't know a lot about him. I've run by more than a few of his pieces since I've been in this business, though. It wouldn't be unheard of for someone around here to have a piece or two by him."

"Well, thanks, anyway. I'll let her know what you said."

Dan handed the locket back to Penelope. "It's beautiful work. A little polish and it would be stunning. Tell her she should wear it."

"I will. Thanks again. I should let you get back to work. It was nice talking to you." She turned to leave.

"Penelope."

She paused. "Yes?"

He took a deep breath. Everything he said next came out in one long exhale. "Maybe you could stop by one day, you know, after the shop closes, and we could go out for dinner somewhere?"

She stared at him, a little shocked. Was he asking her out on a date? The words tumbled out of her mouth before she could stop them. "Sure. That sounds great. When?"

"How about Thursday?" He pointed to the store window.

"Store closes at five."

She nodded. "I'll be here."

She turned to leave again, this time with her stomach tied in knots.

Detective Jim Everett stared at his desk. In front of him rested a neat stack of files. He'd gone through each of them at least a dozen times, hoping for some other explanation than the one he arrived at again and again. Evidence tampering. Fourteen cases spanning more than ten years. And the only person who could have done it was Jonathan Drake, Penny's father.

Jonathan had once been a close friend. It was bad enough to think he could have been a dirty cop, but something truly weird was going on with these cases, something that raised the hairs on the back of Jim's neck, like a quiet whisper in a dark room. Strange circumstances surrounded each one, whether it was a murdered woman with an odd symbol cut into her arm or a missing person who seemingly vanished from a moving car. Also, every evidence box was misplaced in a unique and creative way, and when Jim opened each of them, he discovered a small scrap of paper inscribed with a five-pointed star and other symbols, plus a cache of dried herbs.

Jim was a good Christian. He'd gone to church his entire life. He knew just about every hymn in the hymnal by heart, at least the first, second, and fourth stanzas. He believed the Bible was the literal Word of God, and the Bible said the Devil was real. The drawings on those pieces of paper looked Satanic to him, but Jonathan Drake didn't exactly fit the profile of a Satan worshipper. He was a good man from a good family. Penny Drake was like Jim's own daughter.

Nothing made sense.

Jim never told anyone that when Jonathan left the police force, he'd kept Jonathan's rolodex. Now he thought going through Jonathan's old contacts might help him get to the bottom of things. He had to start somewhere, after all. Flipping through, he found a lot of the same names in his own rolodex, but a few stood out as unusual—a professor of anthropology at Furman University, a self-styled psychic with an office address in Greer, a pastor at a small AME church.

As he reached for the phone to give the college professor a call, the rolodex flipped on its own, to a card he hadn't seen before. All it contained was a name, an address, and a phone number, no job title or other information. The name, Margaret Delacorte, he didn't recognize, but the smell that rose from the card—sage and ash and something slightly coppery, like blood—was familiar. The same aroma hit him when he opened each of the evidence boxes.

Jim dialed the phone number.

Charles' phone rang. He let it go. He was busy. He smoothed out the leather he had just glued to a piece of cardboard that would become the new cover of a book. After the glue dried, he'd stamp the name into the leather and add gold leaf. Normally, he wouldn't go to so much trouble for one of his books. He didn't need them to be fancy. He just wanted to repair them. This one was special, though. It belonged to Millie.

His jaw dropped when he saw it on a shelf in her Harlem apartment. He recognized it as one of the books he got from Roy Arnold. It must have fallen into the rogue magician's hands somehow. When Charles leafed through it, he discovered it was a book of everyday folk magic, written in a peculiar French patois. Millie told him the book had belonged to her grandmother. When she died, she wanted Millie to have it. Millie thought it was just an old recipe book. She didn't understand the true meanings of the "recipes" written down in it.

The book could very well have been tethering Millie's spirit to the present, but he hadn't worked out exactly why or how he was being drawn into her world of Jazz Age Harlem. All he knew at the moment was that he wanted her book to be perfect.

Libraries made Zed nervous. He and Jake sat in a stiflingly quiet room on the second floor of the Greenville County Public Library, looking through every book and record they could find about graveyards in the Low Country.

The library outing was Jake's idea. He figured if they looked at enough pictures, one of them might trigger something, enough to identify the place they saw in their shared vision of the future. Given the sheer number of dead people who had accumulated in the last several hundred years, though, there was a lot of ground to cover, and so far, they'd come up empty.

Zed slammed shut the book on the table in front of him a little too hard, earning dirty looks from the only other person in the room, an older man with wisps of white hair surrounded by a fort he'd built from books about the Civil War.

Jake glanced across the table at Zed. "Something the matter?"

Zed rested his chin in his hands. "I don't know. I just can't help but feel like we're wasting our time here."

"What would you suggest we do instead?" Jake shut the book he'd been looking through. "I don't want to wait for what I—we—saw to happen this time."

Jake was right. At least they were doing something. Zed just hated feeling so toothless against the bad guys. He'd been beaten senseless by Roy Arnold, even if Arnold did have a demon inside him at the time, and he hadn't been much help against Patrick Wheeler either. Charles deserved the credit for that one, mostly, although he claimed the rock that bashed in the side of Patrick Wheeler's head wasn't his doing.

And now here was Jake, all curly brown hair and square jaw and tight polo shirts. He didn't ask to get tangled up in Zed's business. If anything happened to him …

After a glance at their elderly companion, Zed leaned across the table. "I've been meaning to ask you something."

Jake raised an eyebrow. "What?"

"When you were coming to last night, it sounded like you said, 'happiness.' Do you have any idea what that was about?"

Jake shook his head. "Not at all. I don't even remember saying anything. What do think that means?"

Zed shrugged. "I don't have a clue. I didn't see anything to be happy about. That's for damn sure."

Jake opened his book again. "I've been thinking. The cemetery we saw seemed overgrown and neglected."

"So, it probably isn't attached to a church, at least not an active one. Another thing, too. The markers themselves were pretty plain. Some of them didn't even have names."

"What does that mean?" Jake asked.

"Have you ever seen some of the fancy gravestones in the Christ Church cemetery? Some of those mausoleums are bigger than my apartment. We're not looking for a place where rich people are reposing in their eternal slumber—a family plot maybe, or a graveyard for blacks."

After the Civil War, blacks were still buried separately, not fit even in death to share the same space with whites. It made Zed's blood boil every time he thought about things like that. Racism was such a stupid, evil, vile human invention. After all, boiling or otherwise, everyone's blood was the same color.

"That narrows our search down a little," Jake said.

"But not nearly enough."

Jake's gaze went to the stack of books on the table. "It's going to have to be enough."

Never in a million years would Penelope have guessed who decided to come calling that afternoon. When she answered the door, she was met with the frowning face of the Reverend Lowell Purdue. Despite his best efforts to appear quite literally holier than thou, the dark circles under his eyes and his slumped shoulders betrayed him. He was tired, and maybe a little afraid, and also angry.

"Miss Drake, may I come in?" he asked.

She eyed him warily, but stepped aside so he could enter. "Of course."

She ushered him into her office and offered him a chair.

"What can I do for you today, Reverend Purdue?" she asked as she sat down behind her desk, putting a physical barrier between her and the preacher.

She had the feeling they would both be more comfortable that way.

He looked around, scowling as if he might lose his salvation just by being there. "You said you were friends with a member of my congregation, Patrick Wheeler."

Reverend Purdue had been a thorn in her side during their initial encounter with Wheeler. Somehow Wheeler had weaseled his way into the congregation of the Little Rock Southern Baptist Church, and Penelope was more than certain he had a lot to do with the protests the church had staged at the Brown warehouse, even if the good preacher was the one barking Bible verses into a megaphone.

Penelope nodded. "I did say that."

A lie, a necessary one at the time. She just hoped she remembered all the details.

"He hasn't been in church in some time now, since you paid us a visit, actually. I was just wondering if you'd heard from him at all. I—we miss him and are a little worried." He paused between words, choosing them carefully.

"Sorry, I haven't heard from him in a while," Penelope replied.

Because he's buried behind an old farmhouse out in the middle of nowhere.

Reverend Purdue sighed. "Well, if you do, let him know we all at the Little Rock Southern Baptist Church miss him and would love to see him back in the pews."

He motioned to get up. Penelope remained in her chair.

"Reverend Purdue," she said, "with all due respect, you didn't pay me a personal visit just to ask me about Patrick Wheeler. You could have done that with a phone call. And it must be something truly important if you're willing to risk a visit to the house of an unmarried woman without a chaperone."

The preacher pursed his lips and slumped back into the chair. "How well did you know Patrick?"

Penelope didn't see any other choice but to keep the lie going. Bearing false witness to a preacher should have made her feel guiltier than it did. "Well, I can't say we were close, but I cared about him as a friend."

He glanced down. His hands rested in his lap, palms

pressed together. When he looked back up at her, he smiled, clearly uncomfortable. He really must not have wanted to ask the next question. "Would you say he is a person quick to anger?"

"If I recall, you described him as a fine Christian young man," Penelope responded.

The preacher's nostrils flared, but otherwise, he kept his anger in check. "I stand by what I said, but Patrick did struggle with his own personal stumbling blocks, like all of us do."

"His father did commit suicide when he was a teenager," Penelope said. "That had to have left some scars. I may have seen him get angry once or twice, but nothing out of the ordinary. Why do you ask?"

He took a deep breath. "Miss Drake, are you familiar with 1 Peter 5:8?"

She barely managed to keep from rolling her eyes. "Why don't you refresh my memory?"

"'Be sober, be vigilant; because your adversary the devil, as a roaring lion, walketh about, seeking whom he may devour.'"

"So, you believe the Devil devoured Patrick?"

His eyes narrowed. "I have the sense you're mocking me, Miss Drake, but there is a lot of truth in what you say. I think Patrick's anger may have allowed Satan to influence him, and our church."

"So, you admit your publicity stunt at the Brown warehouse was wrong?"

Reverend Purdue shifted in his seat. "That was no stunt, and that is not what I meant."

"What do you have against the Browns, Reverend Purdue?"

"They do not make their money honestly."

Penelope let out a chuckle. "Neither do lawyers, but

you're not protesting any law firms from what I've seen."

"They made a bargain with Satan, Miss Drake, and it appears he's come to collect."

"What do you mean by that?"

"I come from a long line of farmers. There have been stories about the Browns going on three generations now. Their good fortune has at times been ... improbable, and people who cross them have a habit of coming to bad ends."

"That hardly means they've made a pact with the Devil."

He took another deep breath. "There is more to this story, Miss Drake. Patrick told me his father's suicide had to do with something Ephraim Brown did to ruin him financially."

That was a lie. Patrick's family wasn't even from Greenville.

"When I heard about the Satanic activity at the Brown warehouse, I knew it was no coincidence Patrick had joined our congregation," Reverend Purdue continued. "God was calling us to take action, but in the end, Patrick's own anger may have blinded him to our mission as a church."

"Spreading God's love?" Penelope offered.

He looked at Penelope like an indulgent parent. "Spreading God's whole message. Love and mercy, yes, but also His judgment."

"I'm pretty sure the judgment part came through loud and clear."

If he picked up on her sarcasm at all, he ignored it. "Patrick wanted us to do more than show light on the Devil's work, though. In his last conversation with me, he talked about wanting to do more to the Browns to hurt them. He mentioned breaking into the warehouse. Naturally I counseled against that."

Penelope did her best to keep her temper in check. "You knew this when we talked before. Why didn't you tell me any of it then? Or go to the police?"

Reverend Purdue held up his hands. "It wasn't my place. He spoke to me in confidence."

"So, what's happened?" Penelope asked. "What has changed since then that you're coming to me now?"

"You know how the Holy Spirit endows those who believe with spiritual gifts."

"I believe I had a Sunday School lesson about that at one point."

"Such a shame your church doesn't put more emphasis on such things, given that we are called to use our gifts to fight against the darkness every day. Spiritual gifts are not to be taken lightly, Miss Drake."

Penelope was getting tired of these games. "What is your point, Reverend Purdue?"

"One of those gifts is the gift of prophecy."

She raised an eyebrow. "Prophecy? Is that one of your spiritual gifts?"

He nodded. "Over the last several weeks, I have been plagued with dreams. I've asked about you and your family, Miss Drake, and I've discovered quite a bit—more than I expected. I don't believe you'll as easily dismiss what I'm about to say as the police might."

"So, what have you seen in these dreams?"

"I can see Patrick standing somewhere in the woods. His clothes are all black. Somewhere nearby there's a house."

Penelope took in a quick breath. She hoped the Reverend didn't notice.

"I can feel his pain and anger," the Reverend continued. "He's trying to tell me something, but I can't hear. It gets dark, but not like it does when the sun sets. The darkness instead comes rushing through the woods. It overtakes Patrick, washes over him like a giant wave. I run, but there's nowhere to go. Somehow, I know that even if I can reach the house, the person who lives there won't let me in. In the end, it doesn't matter, though. I don't get to the house in time. The darkness surrounds me. I can't see anything. It's cold, and I know I'll never know the warmth of the sun again. In that darkness I can hear one word being whispered over and over again. *Happiness.*"

While he talked, the mask fell off completely. Gone was the arrogant preacher, certain in his faith, sure of his salvation and his moral superiority, replaced by someone scared of something he couldn't understand, couldn't control.

Unfortunately for him, Penelope wasn't in the mood to offer reassurances. She was too busy trying to guess the meaning of the dream and how much trouble they were in if any part of Patrick Wheeler's spirit had managed to linger.

"Did you come here to hire me, Reverend Purdue?" she asked.

He glanced down at his hands in his lap again. "I want you to find Patrick."

"And who would be paying me? You or the Little Rock Southern Baptist Church?"

"Your fee would be paid entirely by me personally."

She shook her head. "I'm sorry, but that's not a job I can take right now."

His face contorted in an angry scowl. "Why not?" There it was again. The pride. He jutted out his chin. "I'm sorry, I thought you cared about your friend. Did I get that wrong?"

"You didn't get that wrong at all. I care. I just don't have the resources right now to dedicate to the case. Finding people takes a lot of effort."

She considered taking his money for a fraction of a second, but she couldn't do it in good conscience. There certainly needed to be an investigation, just not the one the preacher thought.

"The dreams need to end." His voice trembled.

Penelope held her ground. "I'm sorry. I can't help you with that."

The Reverend's expression hardened. "Thank you for your time, Miss Drake. I won't trouble you anymore. You have a blessed day."

With a curt nod, he stood and left. Penelope glanced down at the painted paperweight on her desk. Her father would have known how to handle that situation better. Maybe he could have helped, too, to figure out the meaning behind the Reverend's dreams. The daemons in Patrick Wheeler's service took pleasure is spreading hopelessness and despair. Why would the voices in the darkness whisper the word *happiness*?

All the lights were off when Bertram pulled into the driveway. He didn't think anything about it. After all, it was almost midnight. He hadn't meant to get home so late, but he'd run into an old college buddy on his way out of Asheville. He'd invited Bertram over to his place for a beer, which turned into several, and, well, there he was.

After he managed to get his housekey in the lock on the fourth try, Bertram pushed the door open and stumbled inside. Everything was still. Sometimes his dad stayed up late, but he'd apparently decided to go to bed early that evening. Bertram's talk with his father would have to wait. Again.

As he shambled toward the stairs, though, a flicker of something from the back of the house caught his attention. His left hand automatically went to the charm bracelet circling his right wrist, his fingers seeking out the comfort of the bracelet's texture. Strands of leather wove around small stones, silver charms, and other objects Bertram preferred not to think about. The bracelet was supposed to protect him from malicious magic. He hoped it hadn't lost any juice.

Silence smothered the house like a blanket. Bertram moved down the hallway toward the family room. The air grew stale, oppressive, bad-tasting even, like rotten fruit. He glanced into the kitchen as he passed. Dirty dishes filled the sink, and empty beer bottles littered the counter. That was a little unusual. He'd never considered his dad a slob.

Bertram paused in the doorway to the family room. The television was on with the volume turned all the way down. The screen showed only static. Could that have been the flicker of movement he saw? The dancing gray light threw an eerie glow onto his dad's leather recliner.

Bertram stepped into the room. "Dad? Dad, did you fall asleep watching TV?"

He went to turn the television off, expecting to see his dad slumped over in the recliner, but the chair was empty. Bertram scanned the room. Nothing else seemed amiss, until he noticed the back door ajar. A shaft of moonlight spilled into the room through the gap.

Bertram's heart pounded in his chest. He crept toward the door. When he reached it, he placed a tentative hand on the door knob. He glanced back over his shoulder at the dark and empty family room before he pulled the door open just enough to peer out into the back yard. The moon gave off enough light to see the whole thing—the kidney-shaped pool, the patio with the grill and the fire pit—everything for a child's dream summer.

But he wasn't a kid anymore.

And summer was over.

His dad wasn't in the back yard either, but the feeling something was wrong intensified. Without thinking about it too much, Bertram slipped through the door and outside onto the patio. The eerie silence struck him there, too. Normally he'd be hearing crickets and owls and the rustle of leaves in the breeze, but there was nothing.

The fire pit attracted his attention. All the patio chairs normally around it were shoved to one side. As Bertram approached the pit, he caught a faint whiff of herbs like sage and rosemary and mustard, and he wondered why his dad was using the fire pit to cook instead of the grill, but then other aromas assaulted his nose—the smell of tar and something distinctly coppery.

When he saw the rim of the fire pit he finally understood. All around it symbols and words were drawn in chalk. The bile rose in his throat. Bertram backed away so fast he nearly tripped over his own feet. His thoughts went to the pentagram drawn on the floor of the warehouse before it was destroyed. Daemons had been responsible for that, and back in August daemons had come for him in that very back yard. At the edges of his vision, the shadows moved. He turned and broke into a run. He practically dove through the back door, slamming it shut behind him.

A search upstairs confirmed his fears. His dad wasn't there.

But something else was.

While he stood in his parents' room, a figure appeared in the mirror, leering at him with green eyes and a grinning mouth full of pointed teeth. He bolted down the stairs and out the front door. He swore he heard laughter and felt sharp fingernails scrape down his back as he burst outside. The tires screeched as he pulled his Camaro out of the driveway. He wasn't sure where he was going. All he knew was that he had to get away from there or he wasn't going to see another sunrise.

On December 31, 1919, the Blue Club threw one hell of a New Year's Eve party. It would be the very last one before Prohibition went into effect in January 1920. Lewis pulled out all the stops. Oysters, steaks, whole roasted pheasants, and everything in between, and of course, buckets of champagne. Despite the cold weather, the room was burning up. The band played, and people danced, and for just one night, they forgot all their cares.

Charles couldn't afford to forget, though. He never stopped moving, making sure the night went off without a hitch. Whenever Millie came on stage, he always managed to steal a moment or two to listen to her sing, but that night he couldn't spare even a second. He took comfort in the fact that he could see her later, after the turn of the new year and all the revelers stumbled home.

It was almost two in the morning before he got a chance. Charles approached Millie's dressing room and was about to knock when he heard talking on the other side. Millie's melodious voice was easy to pick out. The other voice was lower—a man. Charles stepped back and retreated to the main room where he sat down at the bar. The clatter of dishes and glasses from the kitchen told him the dishwashers were still cleaning up, but otherwise everyone had gone home, even Lewis.

Soon the door to the backstage opened, and Andre Lestrade, Lewis' new business partner, emerged. He had purchased a share of the club about a month earlier. Charles didn't like it. Already he was making changes—firing long-term employees and bringing in his own people, reserving tables for "important" friends with unsavory reputations. Not to mention the checks Charles saw made out to names he didn't recognize.

Lewis said everything was above-board, and it was all

good for business, but Andre's business was crooked in every way. Most of all, though, Charles really didn't like the way Andre looked at Millie. Millie, for her part, said she could take care of herself, and under any other circumstance, Charles would have agreed, but no one said no to a man like Andre Lestrade. If he wanted something, he got it, one way or another.

Andre waved to Charles. "What are you still doing here, Isaiah? Go home. Get some sleep. You deserve it after the night we just had. Everything went off without a hitch thanks to you, and no one who was here tonight can say they didn't have a blast."

Charles forced a smile. "Given the amount of liquor we went through, I'll say. I suppose we won't be having any more nights like that."

He slapped Charles on the back. "Oh, I wouldn't worry too much about that. We've got big plans for the Blue Club."

Charles eyed him. "What sort of plans?"

Andre wagged a finger. "Not just yet. When the time is right, Lewis and I are planning to bring you on board. You'll see, then. It'll knock your socks off."

"Yeah, Andre, we'll see. I don't plan on going anywhere anytime soon."

Andre laughed as he left through the front door, letting in a blast of chilly winter air. Briefly, Charles thought about going to see Millie, but he changed his mind and left himself, walking the few blocks to his apartment in the cold January night.

Millie came by his apartment at about four o'clock the next afternoon. She didn't say anything when he opened the door. She didn't need to. He just stepped out of the way as she came inside.

"You didn't stop by my dressing room to see me," she said.

Charles closed the door. "I did, but you already had company."

"Nothing happened, Isaiah. You know that."

"I know. But why was he there? Why was he talking to you? Why are you keeping me in the dark about things?" He sighed and pinched the bridge of his nose. "I'm the manager. I should know about what's going on before you do."

She glared. "Why? Because I'm just a singer?"

"I didn't say that."

"But you meant it."

He reached over to caress her shoulder. "Millie, you are amazing, and I don't doubt you could be President of the United States if you set your mind to it, but *my* job is managing the Blue Club, and I can't do *my* job if I don't know what's going on."

She placed her hand atop his. "Andre just wanted to talk to me about a party he's throwing in a couple of weeks for some friends of his. He wants me to give a little private performance and asked me to sing some of his favorite songs. That's all. I promise."

Charles jerked away. "Is this party going to be at the Blue Club? Are we going to have to close down again? That's the fourth time in two months. Do you know how much money we lose every time he does that? We can't afford to lose anymore, especially with all the liquor drying up. People don't get all dolled up to come out and drink water."

She blinked, clearly stung by his words. "I thought you said people would come out to hear me sing in an empty warehouse. Now you're saying all they want is to drink?"

Charles silently cursed himself for letting his temper get

the best of him. "I didn't mean it that way."

"Then why did you say it that way?" she asked. "Besides … I don't think you need to worry."

He snorted. "Now you sound like Andre."

But the downcast expression on Millie's face told him what he already suspected.

"Wait," he said. "Lewis and Andre aren't planning to stop selling liquor, are they?"

She shook her head.

Charles threw his hands up. "What are they thinking? That's crazy."

"See, they knew you'd be this way. That's why they didn't want to tell you at first." She cocked an eyebrow. "Really, you think it's just the Blue Club? Every jazz joint in Harlem is doing the same thing."

"How do they plan on not getting caught?"

"There's a big room in the basement," Millie replied. "It was just used for storage. They made it into a secret bar."

Dozens of odd little things that had happened over the last month suddenly fell into place. "Those workers I let in a few weeks back—"

"You thought they were just here to work on the accountant's office on the floors above the club?"

Charles felt stupid for not adding things up sooner. "So, you've got a secret bar. How are you getting the liquor there? And who's making it if it's illegal?"

She shrugged. "I'll leave that to Lewis and Andre. I would suggest you do the same."

He shook his head. "This isn't right, Millie."

She frowned. "Why are you so opposed to this? Why do you care so much?"

"I told you, Millie. Andre is bad news. Nothing good is going to come from getting mixed up with him."

"You're just overreacting. I can handle him."

He shook his head. "But that's not all I'm worried about. You get mixed up in the things he's mixed up in, you're bound to make enemies, not to mention what happens if the police get on his tail. Or the FBI. I don't want to see anyone hurt, especially not you."

"Why would I get hurt?"

Because the obituary your ghost showed me says you're going to die three months from now.

But he couldn't say that.

"I keep telling you I can take care of myself." She took a step closer. "And whatever I can't take care of, I know you can, now that you're here."

Now that you're here.

What did she mean by that?

"You act like you were expecting me to show up or something."

She pulled at his shirt collar. "Maybe I was. Maybe I've been waiting a long time for you to come into my life, Isaiah Jenkins."

He smelled the sweet roses of her perfume, and for just a moment, his anger faded. When her lips met his, he leaned into the kiss, never wanting it to end.

3.

PENELOPE WOKE UP TO SOMEONE banging on her front door. The clock next to her bed said it was a little after three in the morning. She got up and hurried down the stairs, pulling on a robe as she went and clutching the Louisville Slugger she kept at her bedside. Her charm bracelet didn't give off any warnings, so no dark magic was at play, but neither was there when a brick smashed her office window.

Whoever was on the other side of the door was getting more panicky by the second, calling for her by name. She recognized the voice.

"Penelope. It's Bertram. Please let me in."

When she opened the door, Bertram nearly ran her over trying to get inside.

"Bertram, what—"

"Shut the door. Hurry. Shut it!"

She did as she was told. "Bertram what's going on?"

Bertram stood in the middle of the foyer, wild-eyed, hands shaking, struggling to catch his breath. His gaze darted around the room. "They followed me here."

"Who?"

Bertram gestured frantically toward the door. "Those things. The daemons. They were following the car."

"Daemons? You saw them."

"I didn't have to see them. I know they were there." His words had a hard edge to them.

A daemon had possessed Bertram's body in order to commit at least one murder, something they'd managed to cover up so far. It was all part of Patrick Wheeler's evil plan. Seeing Bertram so agitated made Penelope wonder just how much of a toll being possessed by one of those dark creatures had taken on him.

"Bertram, what's going on?"

"Dad's gone. Missing."

An icy ball of dread formed in Penelope's stomach. "When?"

He ran his fingers through his hair. "I don't know. I've been out of town for a couple of days. I got home kind of late. The house was dark. The door was open to the back yard. I found some … upsetting things there. The daemons were there, too, waiting. They must have taken Dad."

"Upsetting things? What kind of upsetting things did you find?"

"One of those spells like Charles does. There were weird symbols drawn all around the fire pit, and it smelled like when we got baked at parties back in college, only about a thousand times worse."

Penelope shook her head. "I never got baked in college."

He shot her a dirty look. "You know what I mean. When the daemons showed up, it scared the shit out of me. I didn't know where else to go, so I came here. Sorry I woke you up."

"It's fine." She put on what she thought was a reassuring

smile. "We can go back over there when the sun comes up and take a look around. Charles and Zed might be able to help, too."

Chewing his lip, Bertram stared at the baseball bat Penelope still held. "So, does that mean I can …"

She set the Louisville Slugger down by the door. "Stay here? Of course. Guest room is all yours if you want to try to get some sleep."

His whole body slumped in relief. "Thanks."

Penelope grasped his hand. "We'll find your dad, Bertram. I promise."

Bertram staggered out of the bedroom at around ten in the morning, still looking like he'd been run over by a truck. Penelope was sitting on the couch, reading a trashy true crime paperback. She shut it quickly and stuffed it between the cushions.

"Coffee's in the kitchen if you want some," she said.

Long ago, the old house had been divided into two apartments, one upstairs and one downstairs. Her father had converted the downstairs apartment into his office when he became a private detective. They lived together in the apartment upstairs until he died. Now Penelope lived there alone.

Bertram yawned. "It's going to take a lot more than coffee to get me through today, I think."

"Got plenty of bourbon, too."

"I might take you up on that." He walked into the kitchen, scooped up the mug Penelope had set out for him, and poured himself a cup of brown sludge.

"How are you holding up?" she asked.

"Been better. I used the phone in the bedroom to call my mom just now. She's still in Virginia, staying with a cousin of hers. I promise I'll pay the long-distance charge."

"Did you tell her about your dad?"

"No. I'm not going to do that unless I absolutely have to. There's no point in upsetting her more." He threw himself down on the couch next to her. "I did ask her about the last time she talked to Dad, though."

"And?"

Bertram stared into his coffee mug. "She said she hasn't spoken with him in more than a week."

"So, nothing helpful there."

He shook his head. "You don't understand. They've never gone more than a couple of days without talking to each other. They're not estranged. My mom has just been staying with relatives because she still has problems with our house, you know after what happened."

Louise Brown had been possessed by a spirit trapped in a cursed brooch, part of Roy Arnold's elaborate scheme of revenge. They had saved her and taken care of the rogue magician, but then the trouble with Patrick Wheeler started up. Penelope didn't realize it at first, but she had spent the last couple of months waiting for the final shoe to drop. The story of the Brown family wasn't over yet.

"Maybe they had a fight," she offered.

"No, Mom was as puzzled as I was. Dad just stopped calling, and he didn't pick up whenever she called him."

"Any idea why?"

Bertram took a sip of coffee, made a face, and took another sip anyway. "He's been acting strange the last few weeks. He had this weird glint in his eyes, and he talked about fixing everything, making things even better than they were before."

Knowing what she knew about Ephraim's secret talent for magic, Penelope didn't like the inferences to be made there.

"How so?"

Bertram shrugged. "Hell if I know. He never would tell me anything when I asked. He just said he was taking care of things. I can't imagine how. We don't have the funds to rebuild the warehouse and replace what we lost, and the insurance company's been dragging their feet. I think they suspect the explosion that blew up the warehouse wasn't exactly an accident, but I really don't believe they'd be willing to accept a demon-possessed tractor as an explanation."

Just then there was a knock at the front door. Muttering under her breath about Grand Central Station, Penelope went to answer. She found Zed on her front porch. He didn't look like he'd gotten much sleep either. He raised an eyebrow when he came upstairs and saw Bertram in the kitchen pouring himself a second cup of coffee, but he didn't say anything. He simply nodded in Bertram's direction. Bertram saluted back with his coffee mug.

"Coffee?" Penelope asked.

Zed shook his head. "No, thanks."

"You sure?" Bertram took a big gulp and grimaced. "You're missing out."

Zed ignored him. "Penelope, there's something we need to talk about. This business with Patrick Wheeler, I don't think it's over yet."

Penelope exchanged glances with Bertram. "You don't say?"

Zed frowned as his gaze passed between the two of them. "What's going on?"

Penelope turned toward Bertram. "You want to tell him? You were there."

Bertram sketched out the events of the night before for Zed, from discovering his father was missing to being chased by daemons through the streets of Greenville. As Zed listened, he grew a shade paler.

"Funny you should mention daemons," Zed said when Bertram finished, though he wasn't smiling. "I've been having dreams about them chasing me through the woods, and I don't think they're your average run-of-the-mill nightmares."

"What makes you say that?" Penelope asked.

Zed scrunched up his face. "I don't know. They just seem like more. They're too real to be just dreams."

Penelope had the impression he was holding something back.

Bertram set his empty mug down on the counter a little too hard, the noise echoing through the tiny kitchen. "I thought we'd taken care of Patrick Wheeler. Charles said he couldn't come back." He tried to hide his trembling hand behind his back.

Penelope noticed. "Why don't I call Charles? Hopefully he can meet us at your parents' house, and we can all put our heads together to figure out what's going on."

Zed huffed. "Let's all just hope Charles decides to answer the phone."

Upon hearing a knock at his door, Charles' first thought was that he needed to strengthen the wards again. Maybe this time he'd do more than just shore up the barriers protecting his property from anyone—or anything—that might wish him ill. He'd recently stumbled upon a book written by a hermit monk who lived in the mountains of Lombardy in the fifteenth century. The book's spine was damaged, and when Charles picked it up, it fell open to an intriguing spell. The incantation scribbled out in cramped Latin could put the notion in a person's head that they just didn't want to pay him a visit at all. Charles found the idea tempting, but messing with people's heads could have all kinds of unforeseen consequences.

The knocking persisted, and despite his better judgement, Charles went to answer the door. An older man dressed in a suit stood on the porch, maybe in his early sixties, not fat but well-fed.

"Can I help you?" Charles hoped his frown would do what magic failed to accomplish.

The man smiled, not a genuine smile, but one calculated to put Charles at ease, one meant to make him let his guard down. "Good morning. My name is Jim Everett. I'm looking for someone named Margaret Delacorte. Does she happen to be home?"

Charles shook his head. "She doesn't live here anymore."

The man seemed taken aback, as if he hadn't considered that possibility. "Do you know where she might have moved to?"

"She's dead."

Again, that same confused look. "Oh, I see. I'm so sorry. Are you … are you her son?"

Charles nodded. "More or less."

The furrow of his brow deepened, and the corner of his mouth twitched. Everett's confusion was growing, and so was his annoyance. "What does that mean?"

"My name is Charles. Margaret adopted me when I was small. She raised me. Any particular reason you're looking for her?"

Everett glanced past him, into the front parlor. His gaze took in the bookshelves lining all the walls, laden with books. Charles had recently rearranged them to accommodate the acquisitions from Roy Arnold's hoard. There wasn't any other furniture in the room. Most people would consider the arrangement curious, even suspect. No doubt Everett was making his own judgments.

"Have you ever met anyone by the name of Jonathan Drake?" he asked.

Drake. Penelope's father. It hit Charles where he had heard the man's name before. Jim Everett was a police detective. No good in lying then.

"I've heard of him. What's this about?"

Everett shifted his weight. One foot crossed the threshold. "Can I come in?"

Charles met his gaze. "Is there a reason you need to?"

Detective Everett raised himself up, the color rising in his face. He probably wasn't used to being talked to that way by someone like Charles. He could see the indignation in the detective's eyes, but Charles refused to look away.

The next few moments seemed like hours—enough time for Charles to wonder if he'd pay for exercising his rights— but then the detective's shoulders slumped, and he sighed. "Thank you for your time. I'm sorry to have bothered you. You have a nice rest of your day."

Charles shut the door without replying. He listened to Detective Everett's footsteps on the porch as he retreated back down the steps and through the overgrown yard. Finally, when the crunch of tires on the gravel drive faded into the distance, Charles went to grab his leather satchel. He didn't have time to think about why a police detective would be looking for Margaret after all these years, and asking about Penelope's father, too. That would have to wait for later. He had his own appointment to keep.

As he was leaving through the back door, his telephone rang. He let it go. More and more that spell seemed like a good idea.

When Charles didn't answer the phone, Penelope, Zed and Bertram went ahead to the house on Crescent Avenue without him. Penelope hated that Zed was right. She wanted so desperately to believe Charles had come around finally, that he was ready to include people in his life again, but every time it seemed like he was better, he retreated back into his old habits, isolating himself in that falling-down farmhouse in the middle of nowhere, surrounded by his books, pushing everyone away.

The oversized brick colonial stood silent and dark, unexceptional among the other mansions on Crescent Avenue, revealing no hint anything out of the ordinary had ever happened there. *If the neighbors only knew,* Penelope thought. Bertram led them all straight to the fire pit in the back yard.

"If I didn't know better, I would think the neighborhood teenagers were pulling some kind of prank." He pointed to the lines drawn in a practiced, methodical hand around the fire pit's rim. "But tell me if those don't look like the same symbols as the pentagram from the warehouse."

Zed leaned over and studied the chalk markings, wrinkling his nose at the lingering smell. "Just because some of the symbols are the same doesn't mean this circle was intended to summon a demon."

Bertram frowned. "Then what was it used for?"

"It's hard to tell." Zed pointed to one of the symbols, which looked like an arrow crossed with three diagonal lines. "There are lots of spells that might use these elements. Shapes, symbols, letters, words—they're all just used to focus energy in different ways, depending on how they're combined, depending on where the energy comes from."

Penelope frowned. "Probably safe to say this isn't a cure for a hangover, though, right?"

Zed raised an eyebrow. "If it is, it's major overkill."

"What are you talking about, Penelope?" Bertram asked.

She clenched her fists. "He lied to me."

Bertram crossed his arms. "Who?"

"Your dad, Bertram." She grew more irritated by the second. He should have told her. None of this had to happen. "He practiced magic. He was the one who made the first charm bracelet for you. And the necklace to try to save your mother, or at least keep her calm. He told me he didn't really know how to do much more than cure a hangover, that all he had was a book he inherited from his grandmother. Obviously, he wasn't telling the truth."

"And if he lied about that ..." Zed mumbled.

Bertram scowled. "That's impossible. I've only known about this magic bullshit for a few months. How could he have hidden something like that from me my whole life?"

Zed shook his head. "It's not that hard really. Remember he hid it from your mother, too, and for a lot longer. People don't want to believe in magic, so they ignore or rationalize things. All he would've had to do was tell a few little lies here and there. Your brain just did the rest."

If he had only told the truth, maybe they could have avoided everything that happened. Penelope was mad at Ephraim for lying, but she might have been angrier with herself for taking him at his word. "He's a lot more powerful even than what he admitted to me."

Bertram looked pained as he massaged his temples. "Do you think whatever this is had something to do with the company and all Dad's talk of trying to make things right again?"

Zed dragged his finger through the soot on the lip of the fire pit and brought it up to his nose. He seemed a little on edge. He was sensitive to magic, even if he wasn't a magician himself. Penelope's father had been sensitive to the world beyond the Veil, too. She didn't inherit that trait, so she'd learned to trust Zed's instincts. She was just waiting for him to tell them all to run.

Instead, he wiped his hand on his jeans. "Charles could tell you for sure what this spell was supposed to do, but it doesn't seem like a prosperity spell to me."

Bertram's eye grew wide. "You mean a spell that brings you money? Those things work?"

"Sometimes," Zed replied. "They're not the easiest to pull off. The magic user's motives have to be crystal clear, and when it comes to money, our motives are always so mixed up. But there's a touch of darkness here I'm not so sure about."

Bertram's gaze went to the bushes at the edge of the yard. "The daemons—"

Zed held up a hand. "No, not them. Something else. There's something dark about the spell itself."

Bertram's scowl returned. "Are you telling me my dad was out here practicing some kind of black magic?"

Zed winced at the phrase *black magic*. "I wouldn't throw that term around if I were you, and no, I'm not telling you that at all. A lot of spells intended for good have dark histories and … questionable requirements."

"Care to get any more specific than that?" Bertram inched away from the fire pit.

"I can't. There's definitely something off here, though. I don't like it." Whether consciously or not, Zed also had taken a step back.

The breeze picked up, scattering dead leaves around the yard and stirring the ashes in the fire pit. The wind carried voices—faint whispers.

"Do you have a place to stay, Bertram?" Penelope asked while fixing Zed with her gaze. "I'm not sure you should be here until we figure out what's going on."

Bertram shrugged. "I can find somewhere to crash, I guess."

"You can crash with me," Zed said with a sigh as he glared back at Penelope. "All I can offer is a couch, though."

Bertram glanced back toward the house, as if he expected to see a face staring out at them from one of the darkened windows. "Give me ten minutes to pack a bag."

It seemed to Ephraim as if they'd been walking for hours. Overhead the stars peeked through a web of bare tree branches, black against the indigo blue sky. Leaves crunched under his feet. He shivered. The air was crisp, brittle even, chilly enough to need a jacket, but he didn't have one.

Six of them marched single-file through the woods. He brought up the rear. Up ahead, the light from a flashlight bobbed up and down, dancing like a will-o'-the-wisp from his grandmother's stories of growing up in the mountains, leading them farther into the woods. The light didn't help much with the path directly in front of him, though, and more than once he stumbled over the uneven ground.

He didn't know where he was or what they were all doing there, only that he needed to get control of his growing unease and face down his fear. Otherwise he wouldn't get what he wanted.

But what did he want?

Eventually, they came to a clearing—no, not a clearing. Here and there stones jutted up out of the ground at odd angles. Grave markers. They had arrived at a graveyard, an old and neglected one. Something waited for them there, something ancient, something that wasn't human. A single word echoed through Ephraim's brain.

Happiness.

The fog in Ephraim's head lifted, if only for a moment. He found himself in his bedroom at his grandparents' house. Everything was exactly as he remembered it the last time he'd been there. A patchwork quilt made from old scraps of cloth covered the four-poster bed. A few of his grandmother's cross-stitch samplers hung on the walls. A secretary desk was tucked into one corner, and in another corner, a low chest of drawers stood with a vanity mirror on top. Ephraim paused, shocked at his reflection. Looking back at him was not a gray-haired, middle-aged man with dark circles under his eyes, but a golden-haired boy about ten years old.

Outside the room heavy footsteps made the hardwood floor creak and groan like someone in pain. Ephraim scrambled for somewhere to hide. He had just managed to wriggle himself under the bed when the footsteps stopped directly outside the door. The cut crystal doorknob turned, and the door opened. At the same time the fog returned to Ephraim's brain, and he didn't remember anything else after that.

A general store had stood on the corner of Edgeworth Street and Greenacre Road almost as long as there had been a Nicholtown community. Generation after generation of the Rose family served the mostly black community by stocking things you couldn't get at the Winn-Dixie down the road. Uncommon spices, more unusual cuts of meat, harder-to-find vegetables—any odd ingredient one of your grandmother's recipes called for, Rose's General Store had it.

Charles pulled into the store's tiny parking lot a little before noon. The tailpipe of his pickup truck barked and choked out a plume of black exhaust as he killed the engine.

He grimaced. The last thing he wanted to do was deal with that, but he mentally added it to the already long list of things he had to take care of.

Inside the store an older black man sat on a stool behind the counter. The voice of Lena Horne spilled out of the radio by his elbow. She was singing some lazy blues tune. Charles tried not to think about Millie.

The man, Benjamin Rose, glanced at the clock on the wall behind him. "You're a little late today, Charles."

Charles hoisted his satchel up onto the counter. "Had an unexpected visitor."

"A visitor? You?" Benjamin chuckled.

"Yeah, I wasn't happy about it either."

Benjamin pointed toward the door. "Heard your pickup truck griping again just now, too. You know I got a brother-in-law can—"

"Thanks for the recommendation, but I think I got it covered."

In all honesty the truck was beyond what any mechanic could do for it. Magic held it together more than the rusty nuts and bolts. Charles just needed it to last a little while longer.

"Probably for the best." Benjamin leaned over the counter with a conspiratorial grin. "He's a good-for-nothing SOB anyway. I was just saying something to be nice to my sister."

Charles smiled and shook his head. "You tell Addie I said hello."

"Will do." Benjamin glanced over at Charles' bag. "So, you got anything specific you need today, or are you just looking to resupply?"

"A little bit of both." Charles reached into his satchel, pulled out a notebook, and turned to the page where he'd scrawled out a list of everything he needed to get. It was longer than normal. "I'm looking for some yarrow root. Having the damnedest time finding it anywhere."

Benjamin stroked his chin. "I may have some in the back. Let me go check."

Rose's General Store also catered to those with grocery lists less mundane and more magical, something the Rose family didn't see as anything unusual.

"Magic bleeds through into everyday life," Benjamin told Charles once. "You can't draw a line and say, 'This is magic,' and 'This isn't magic.' People practice magic all the time. They just don't call it that."

All those recipes for tinctures, balms, salves, and teas passed down from generation to generation had a touch of magic in them, and it wasn't really a giant leap from brewing a cure for a headache to mixing up a tonic to make nightmares go away.

While Benjamin was in the back of the store, Charles gathered up the rest of what he needed and brought everything to the counter. Benjamin reemerged from the storeroom holding a small glass jar.

"It's your lucky day." He handed the jar of coarse, brown powder to Charles. "I've only got a little, though. Will that do?"

Charles held the jar up at eye level. "That should be perfect."

"Not a lot of folks around here use yarrow root much. What are you planning on doing with it?"

"It's for something to help me sleep better," Charles answered. "That's all."

Benjamin eyed him. Charles knew what he was thinking. You could go to the drug store to get something to help you sleep better. You didn't need a magic elixir for that. But Charles was telling the truth. He *did* need the yarrow root to help him sleep, just not the way he said it.

Benjamin motioned for Charles to come closer. "Come here. I want to show you something I found. I've been waiting for you to pay a visit."

Benjamin took a package wrapped in brown paper from under the counter. He carefully unfolded the paper to reveal a small wooden box with a hinged top decorated in a pattern of interlocking vines. He opened the top of the box to reveal a deck of tarot cards, the backs emblazoned with the same pattern as the top of the box.

"Like it?" Benjamin took the deck of cards in his hands, thumbing through them to show Charles the illustrations on the faces. "It's from New Orleans, probably printed around 1902."

Charles reached toward the deck. "It's beautiful."

Benjamin gave the deck a quick shuffle and fanned out the cards face down on the top of the counter. "Why don't you pick one?"

"What?" Charles jerked his hand back like he'd gotten an electric shock.

"Pick one," Benjamin repeated. "When was the last time you had any kind of reading done?"

It had been about five years, when Charles was in Vietnam. That reading didn't go well for anyone involved, but he didn't tell Benjamin that. "I don't think this is a good idea."

But Benjamin persisted. "Come on. Just one card."

One card. Not really enough to get a good reading. One card could mean anything at all depending on how you chose to interpret it. How much could Benjamin really find out about Charles from one card?

He sighed. "Okay, fine."

Charles let his fingers hover over the deck for a second, trying to pick up on any malicious magic, but nothing jumped up and tried to bite him. He pulled a card out of the middle and turned it face up on the counter. The card depicted a smiling man seated on a bench in front of a wall. Resting on top of the wall were nine cups.

It was the last card he'd ever expect.

Benjamin started laughing. "The Nine of Cups. The Lord of Happiness. Looks like all your dreams are going to come true."

Charles wasn't in the mood to join in on the laughter. "Maybe not. It's reversed."

Benjamin held up a chiding finger. "Now you know as well as I do the Lord of Happiness is the only card in the deck that's just as lucky reversed as it is right-side-up. Maybe even luckier. That just means you need to look inside yourself for contentedness."

Charles glared. "I think your deck is defective."

"Oh, come on now, Charles. Don't be that way." Benjamin tempered his glee, but the smile never left his face. "Even you've got to let a little happiness into your life sometime. Don't you want your dreams to come true?"

Charles was pretty sure he didn't.

Bertram passed out on Zed's couch around eight o'clock. Zed tried to read a book, but the snoring distracted him. He was about to give up and go to bed himself when there was a knock at his door. He glanced at Bertram sprawled out before he went to answer. Probably Penelope checking on things. Instead, he found Amy Parker, Bobby Parker's sister.

"You decided to knock this time," he said.

The last time Amy visited him, he had found her in his kitchen drinking his coffee, having let herself in. That time she wanted assurances Zed would do his best to get who killed her brother. Zed had kept that promise, after a fashion. He told her the person responsible for her brother's death had been dealt with. She understood what "dealt with" meant and had enough common sense not to ask any more questions. They hadn't talked since, and Zed didn't see any reason they would.

She bit her lip. "I ... need to ask you a favor."

Bertram let out an obnoxious snort before rolling over.

Amy tried to peer past Zed into the apartment. "Is this a bad time?"

"No, it's fine. Just an unexpected houseguest." Zed took a step back. "Come on in. We can talk in the kitchen."

"I don't know anyone else to go to," Amy said once they were both seated at the kitchen table. "Anybody in my family would have me committed."

Zed fished a Winston out of his pocket for himself and offered one to her, too. "What's the problem?"

"I'm getting rid of my grandmother's stuff. I'm tired of tripping over it all the time." She took the cigarette and accepted Zed's light as well. "Bobby was the one who insisted on keeping everything anyway."

When Zed had visited the trailer Amy shared with her brother, uninvited and unannounced, he'd found it crammed to the gills with antique furniture and other things. Their grandmother, who had a touch of magic, died in a housefire that spared Amy and Bobby by some miracle. Zed suspected Bobby had some magic talent himself. In the trailer Zed also discovered their grandmother's old books of folk magic, recipe books as Amy called them, and at least one of them had been used recently.

"It's the books. You don't know what to do with the books."

Amy nodded. "I don't want them. I don't have any use for

them, but I know I can't just sell them to anyone."

"No, that wouldn't be a good idea."

Zed watched Amy's internal struggle play across her features. He didn't need his special talent to see her emotions. Anger, embarrassment, and guilt darkened her eyes and wrinkled her forehead.

She abruptly let out a string of expletives. "I hate this. I'm the last person to ask anyone for anything, but will you take them? Please?"

Zed leaned back in his chair. "You want me to take the books?"

"You would know what to do with them."

He gestured toward his tiny living room where Bertram still snored. "In case you hadn't noticed, I don't really have a lot of room."

"But you know people. Surely you can think of someone to give them to. They need to be kept safe."

Zed didn't want the books, but Amy was making it really hard for him to say no. A lot of people disparaged folk magic, saying it wasn't "real" magic just because the people who practiced it didn't have any formal training. Most didn't know Church Latin from Pig Latin and didn't care to learn the difference, but folk magic could be powerful and dangerous. Just like recipes passed down from generation to generation, how things were written down didn't always match how things were actually done. Only, in unpracticed hands, folk magic could create a lot more problems than biscuits that didn't rise right.

Zed took a long drag and blew a stream of smoke out of the side of his mouth. "Okay, I'll take them."

"Great." She smiled, relief radiating off of her. "They're in the car. I'll just go get them."

She had already brought them. Of course.

4.

Thursday, October 26, 1972

AS THE LAST NOTES OF the song played out, Zed switched on his microphone. "You were just listening to 'Black and White' by Three Dog Night. Coming up next, I've got a song from the Eagles that's pretty appropriate for this time of year, if you ask me, but first here's something to think about on this chilly October morning. I know I've got at least a few listeners who care what I say, God only knows why."

Three days a week, from midnight until five in the morning, Zed deejayed at WRXQ, playing whatever he wanted and saying whatever popped into his head. It was a wonder the station owner hadn't fired him yet, except they'd probably never be able to find anyone else willing to take his job.

"I've been thinking a lot lately about fate or destiny or whatever you want to call it," Zed continued. "Just consider the people you meet every day, the ones you pass in your cars, or walking down the street. Most of them you'll never see again, but all it takes is one random event—you turn left instead of right, or leave your house five minutes later than normal—and you cross paths with someone who becomes more than just a stranger. Maybe they become the most important person in your life, and you have no way of knowing who or when or how that will happen. Or why. I certainly don't have all the answers, but I do know this. We were not meant to walk the world alone, any of us, even on a cold October morning when no one has any business being awake."

Amy Parker certainly didn't have any business being awake. She had to be at work by seven, but she couldn't sleep, and so she found herself listening to the radio, telling herself it was just by chance she happened upon Zed's show.

Amy knew she wasn't alone, even though it felt like it at times. She'd known ever since the angels saved her and Bobby from the fire that killed her grandmother. She'd never been much on going to church, but she always believed the angels watched over the two of them.

Until what happened to Bobby.

Maybe what her mother always said was true. Maybe she should have listened to the preachers sooner. Maybe fiddling with magic was against God's will. Maybe that's why the angels didn't protect Bobby from … the thing that killed him.

That was the real reason she wanted to get rid of the books. Since Bobby was gone, the angels were all she had. She didn't want them to leave her too. Strange how thinking of them made her think of Zed McKay. What was it about his voice that caused her to think of the angels? And what was she doing even thinking about a man she'd spoken to a grand total of four times like that? It was ridiculous. Still, she listened until she finally drifted off to sleep.

Penelope pulled up to her grandmother's house at half past two, just as the ending credits of *The Guiding Light* would be scrolling on the television. She knocked and listened as her grandmother got out of her chair in the den and slowly came to the door. That walk became longer and longer as the years went by, but Edith Drake would never ask for help. She'd lived on her own for over two decades. She wasn't about to stop now.

She ushered Penelope in with a smile and made her sit at the kitchen table while she cut a piece of pecan pie and poured a glass of sweet tea. Penelope was content to let her grandmother talk for a while as she enjoyed her pie and sipped her tea. She learned all about the controversy over the election of the current Junior League president, which led to an essay on exactly what her grandmother thought of *those people* who had broken into that office in Washington, D.C., which somehow segued into her recipe for lemon icebox pie.

The biggest news, though, was her ongoing feud with the music minister at church, who continued his efforts to modernize the Sunday morning worship service. While the guitar had been bad enough, apparently the tambourine was a bridge too far.

She shook her head and clicked her tongue, which growing up had always been Penelope's signal to duck and cover. "And all the while that beautiful pipe organ sits unused."

She did have a point there.

She reached across the table and placed her hand on top of Penelope's. "Listen to me, going on about things you don't care anything about. Tell me about you. What has my favorite granddaughter been up to?"

Too much.

"Not a whole lot," Penelope answered.

Her grandmother eyed her. "Oh, surely that's not the

case. You're always going on about how busy you are. Mrs. Atkinson talks about running into you in the library all the time. Mrs. Redding could have sworn it was your car parked across the street from her neighbor's house for several hours last Thursday. And Mrs. McGee saw you just the other day downtown. She would've said hello, but you were going inside that antique shop on Coffee Street."

The CIA had nothing on Edith Drake.

"That's Grayson & Sons," Penelope said. "I know the owner. He's been helping me with a case."

"Oh, yes, I know exactly the one, but if I recall the Graysons don't own the store anymore, do they? It's the boy with the funny last name. When poor Mrs. Styles passed on a few months ago, her daughters sold some things to him. From what I gather, he's very nice, you know, for a Yankee." Her grandmother said the last word at almost a whisper.

"His name is Dan. Dan Kowalczyk." Penelope took a sip of her iced tea, hoping her grandmother wouldn't notice the flush in her cheeks.

"Yes, that's it. And how is your other gentleman friend? Zed McKay, is that his name? Is that short for Zedediah?"

Penelope wasn't sure exactly. He'd always just been Zed. "Zed's my assistant. He helps me with work."

"Well, in any event, he's awfully handsome."

Even her own grandmother … Penelope couldn't help but roll her eyes. "He's also good at his job. And it's nothing like that. Zed and I are friends. He's … not exactly my type."

Her grandmother pursed her lips. "Well, I'm sure you're the best judge of that."

She did not approve of Penelope's job, and unlike everyone else, she was not afraid to speak her mind. The two of them had recently managed to come to an understanding, though. Penelope believed what she did was important, and not just the supernatural cases, but the normal ones, too. People, mostly women, came to Penelope who were afraid to go to the police, or even to other private detectives. Her grandmother disapproved because she worried for Penelope's safety, not because she thought Penelope's job was a waste.

"Although you weren't always such a good judge of things," her grandmother continued, chuckling.

"What do you mean?" Penelope asked.

"Bertram Brown used to follow you around like a lost puppy dog when you two were in high school," she held up a finger, "but you would barely give him the time of day."

Penelope shook her head. "I don't remember that."

Her grandmother looked at her like she'd just said she preferred store-bought pie crust. "You had your head in the clouds all the time. It was obvious to everyone else he had a liking for you."

Penelope thought back to those years, to the interactions she'd had with Bertram in high school, trying to figure out what she'd missed. Could she have been that oblivious? "That can't be right. Bertram? Really?"

All the things Patrick Wheeler said when he invaded her home disguised as Bertram came to mind. Maybe he didn't make it all up. Maybe when the daemon got inside Bertram it saw his secrets and told them to Patrick. Penelope shuddered at the idea.

"Have you talked to Bertram recently?" her grandmother asked. "You used to be such good friends. I'm happy you two were able to reconnect. I just wish it was under better circumstances."

Penelope weighed lying, but given the way the conversation was going, thought better of it. "I talked to him just a few days ago. He seems okay."

On the other hand, a little fibbing might be in order.

Her grandmother frowned. "That's just a nasty business all around. Those poor men who were killed all worked for the Browns, you know. Someone's out to get that family."

Penelope stared across the table. It wasn't a closely held secret that all the men murdered by Patrick Wheeler were Brown employees, but at the same time it wasn't a fact shared widely in the news. Her grandmother would have had to do some more-than-casual digging to find out that information. It seemed Edith Drake was still able to surprise her granddaughter.

"Is there a reason someone might be out to get them?"

Reverend Lowell Purdue said the Browns' good fortune at times seemed improbable, and people who crossed them had a habit of coming to bad ends. Roy Arnold. Patrick Wheeler. Was it so far-fetched someone *else* could be set on revenge against the Browns? Someone who conspired with the others? Penelope didn't like where her thoughts were taking her.

"Well, I don't like to repeat idle gossip, but you don't get to be successful like that without stepping on a few people. I've heard stories. You know I'm not Ephraim Brown's biggest fan, but he's an absolute angel compared to his father. That man was a piece of work. And don't even get me started on Ephraim's grandfather. They're both dead and buried, though. I'm not sure why anyone would go after Ephraim for something *they* did."

Penelope asked herself that question, too. But magic was one topic she knew far more about than her grandmother. Ephraim wasn't as innocent as he made himself out to be, and neither was her father. She couldn't shake the notion that somehow everything was tied to whatever happened in the woods outside Columbia all those years ago, and the only people who could tell her the truth were gone.

Zed didn't know what to expect when he walked into the tiny McGovern for President office. It was barely big enough to fit the furniture—a folding table, two folding chairs, an old leather couch, and a red and orange recliner. Campaign signs took up most of the rest of the space.

That afternoon, three people had also managed to cram themselves into the office, two men and a woman. They all looked up at Zed in unison as soon as he entered. He seemed to have interrupted some heated debate between the two men, one of whom was perched on the arm of the couch while the other sat cross-legged at the opposite end. The woman sat in one of the folding chairs at the table, stuffing envelopes.

"Can I help you?" the man balanced on the arm of the couch asked.

He had shaggy black hair and thick-rimmed black glasses. He was probably younger than Zed. They were all probably younger.

"I'm looking for Jake Dempsey," Zed said. "I thought he might be here."

"He had to step out for a minute," the man replied. "He should be back soon." He gestured to the recliner near the door. "You're welcome to wait if you want."

Zed nodded and took a seat. "Sure."

The two men continued their debate, though a little more subdued. They were arguing about the Watergate scandal. Zed had read a few stories in the newspaper about possible links between the Nixon Administration and the break-in at the Democratic National Headquarters, but he didn't know what would come of it, if anything. As the minutes passed, Shaggy Hair and Glasses got more and more animated, jabbing fingers in every direction and declaring at one point that the President needed to be thrown in jail. The other man, a red-head with a line of freckles across the bridge of his nose, accused him of jumping to conclusions.

The woman seemed oblivious as she took pamphlets off a stack, carefully folded each in thirds, and stuffed them into the envelopes in front of her. Zed caught her eye.

"Are those guys always like this?" he asked.

She twisted her mouth into a wry grin. "Most of the time. Usually it's worse. I'm Linda, by the way."

He saluted. "Zed."

She waved a hand over the pamphlets. "We've got plenty of reading material for you if you're looking for something to pass the time."

Zed shook his head. "No thanks."

"Have you thought about who you're going to vote for in November?"

He laughed and immediately regretted it.

Linda's smile melted. "What's so funny?"

"Nothing. Sorry. I wasn't making fun. It's just, so many people pin so much hope on who the President is, but there are a lot of things even the President can't fix."

"There are a lot of things he *can* fix, though," Linda replied, "like this stupid war. McGovern's promised to get us out of Vietnam entirely. So many of our boys have died, and for what? Don't you think it's time to bring all the soldiers home?"

Tears threatened to spill over onto her cheeks, and the grief radiated off of her so intensely it physically pained Zed. She'd lost someone close to her in some nameless jungle half a world away. He agreed about the Vietnam War, but as horrible as the war was, some things were even more terrifying. He doubted very much McGovern knew how to banish a higher-level demon back to Hell. He smiled weakly and picked up a pamphlet. Linda tucked a piece of her long, straight black hair behind one ear and went back to stuffing envelopes, but Zed spied her looking at him more than once.

After a few more minutes, the door opened, and a shadow appeared over his reading material. He glanced up to see Jake standing there, but he wasn't looking at Zed.

Instead, he glared at the two men. "Hey, Allen, Jeff, aren't you supposed to be helping Linda stuff envelopes?"

The two men both sighed loudly as they reluctantly gave up their places on the couch to join Linda, who cheerfully handed each a stack of envelopes to seal and stamp.

Only then did Jake turn his attention to Zed. "Want to talk outside?"

"Your friends seem nice," Zed said once they were out of earshot of everyone else.

Jake still wasn't smiling. "What are you doing here?"

Anger and fear. The last two emotions Zed expected. "I needed to talk to you."

"No one is supposed to know about you," said Jake through a clenched jaw.

So that's what this was about. "You don't have to tell people the truth. You could just introduce me as your friend. I'm not going to say anything. I promise."

Jake bit his lower lip. "Are you saying we're more than friends?"

"I wouldn't have …" Zed glanced through the window of the campaign office just to make sure Linda, Allen, and Jeff were still busy stuffing envelopes. "I wouldn't have done what I did in the bookstore if I didn't want to be more than just friends."

Jake sighed. The anger subsided, but the fear remained. "You're right. I'm sorry. It's just that this is new territory for me, not just with … what's going on between us, but with my 'medical condition,' we'll call it. I've only shared the first secret about myself with a few other people. I've never shared the second one. I'm trying, but it's hard."

Zed wanted more than anything to reach out and put a hand on Jake's shoulder, but he stopped himself. "Look, I get it, but you can trust me. Okay?"

Jake took in a deep breath and nodded.

"Your 'medical condition' is what I came to talk to you about, though," Zed continued. "I came home this morning from my shift at the radio station and collapsed into bed like I normally do. Usually I'm so tired I go right to sleep, and I don't remember my dreams. Today I did. I was there again, in the woods, wherever we were the other times. You didn't happen to have any weird dreams last night, did you?"

The look on Jake's face told Zed the answer to his question. "Yeah, I had another vision this morning. Full-body spasms. Banged my knee pretty good. Woke up on the bathroom floor."

Again, all Zed wanted to do was touch Jake, to wrap his arms around him and cradle his head on his shoulder. He shoved his hands in his pockets. "You all right?"

Jake shrugged. "I'm fine. I've been hurt worse. What did you see?"

"Lots of trees. Gravestones. Demonic shadows. And something else I hadn't seen before. A sign. It said—"

"Happiness," Jake finished.

"So, you saw it, too."

"Yeah, but I still don't understand what it means."

"I'm beginning to, and I don't like it. I have to find out where this graveyard is."

Jake cocked an eyebrow. "You mean *we*. Wherever it is, we're both there."

Zed absentmindedly twisted his amethyst ring around his finger. "I've been thinking about that. Maybe we try to change the future. You can't protect yourself from the things we've seen. I don't want you to get hurt."

Jake crossed his arms. "And what makes you think you're going to be okay?"

"I don't, but I'm more experienced in dealing with this stuff."

"You don't really have a choice here."

Zed shook his head. "I can't put you in danger like that."

"That's not what I mean, Zed." Jake pressed his palms together. "Please listen to me. I've been dealing with this most of my life. No matter what you try to do, what we both saw *is* going to happen. I can't stop it, and neither can you."

Zed understood. He almost believed Jake, but what good was he if he couldn't protect the ones he cared about? "I still have to try."

Jake threw up his hands. "Suit yourself, but don't be surprised when I say I told you so."

He stepped past Zed.

"Where are you going?" asked Zed.

"Back to work," Jake answered as he kept walking. "Someone's got to save Linda from Allen and Jeff."

"I'm just doing what I think is right," Zed called after him.

Jake paused and turned. "I know. I think you're wrong."

"I need to tell you something," Zed said as he threw himself down in the chair opposite Penelope's desk, "and I need you to trust me and not ask a lot of questions, okay?"

Penelope smirked. "So a normal Thursday around here then."

Zed frowned. "I'm serious."

Penelope did her best to reign in her facial expressions.

"Okay, what is it?"

"I think I know where Ephraim is. I mean, I don't exactly know where, but you remember the graveyard I told you I was having dreams about? Where I was being chased by daemons? Find that graveyard, and I think we'll find Ephraim. It's old and neglected, and based on the grave markers, it could be a cemetery meant for black families. I think it might be somewhere in the Low Country."

"Any particular reason you can think of why you're getting these dreams now?" Penelope asked. "I can think of a couple of cases where that trick would have been helpful."

Zed's gaze went to the floor. "You promised not to ask questions."

Penelope regarded him for a moment. Was he afraid? She probably would be, too, in the same situation. "Okay, fine. Just one more question. Why do you think this graveyard is in the Low Country?"

"The woods around it don't look like the woods here," he replied. "I remember there being palmetto trees, for one."

Her father's reassuring knocks still hadn't returned, but Penelope could almost hear them in her head, rapping off replies to her silent questions as she worked through what Zed was telling her. "You know, palmetto trees don't grow just in the Low Country. They grow in Columbia, too, because of the sandy soil. If this is all tied to what happened in college with Ephraim and my dad, then I'll bet you this graveyard is there."

Zed shook his head. "Still, that's a lot of ground to cover. And as neglected as this graveyard looked, it might have been forgotten completely. How would we find it if that's the case? Unless …"

"Unless what?"

Zed lowered his voice, almost to a whisper. "Happiness."

Penelope's blood ran cold. *Happiness* was the word the Reverend Lowell Purdue heard in his nightmare vision of Patrick Wheeler. "What are you talking about?"

"I saw the word on a sign in my last dream. It must mean something. There's no way it doesn't, right?"

"I think it means everything." Penelope jumped out of her chair and beckoned for Zed to follow her. "Come on. We don't have a lot of time."

"Where are we going?" Zed asked.

Penelope was already headed for the door. "To see a friend of my father."

Zed wasn't exactly sure what he expected. The owner of an occult shop maybe. Or a psychic who did readings for people out of her living room. When they parked behind a classroom building on the Furman University campus, Zed shot Penelope a puzzled look. A few minutes later he found himself in a cramped office, face to face with a small woman wearing large, round glasses, her long gray hair plaited in a braid. The brass nameplate on the door said "Dr. Evelyn Boyd."

"I haven't seen you since your father's funeral, Penelope," said the professor. "I hope you're doing okay."

Penelope nodded. "I'm doing fine."

"Well, good. I'm glad to hear it. So, what brings you here today? I assume this is more than just a social call." The professor eyed Zed, who leaned on the wall next to the door, trying to casually hide his discomfort over the number of magically charged artefacts cluttering the space.

Penelope hesitated before she replied. "I know you helped my father in the past with some of his cases."

Penelope was being cautious, unsure how much Professor

Boyd knew about the kinds of cases her father had handled, but among the notebooks and papers strewn on her desk, Zed noticed a working *gris-gris* bag. He also spotted an earthenware pot like the ones he'd seen in houses up in the mountains, meant to contain water from the last snow of the season, and a twist of dried tobacco leaves bound with a white string. Zed was pretty confident Professor Boyd understood more about the unseen world than most, and she knew exactly what Jonathan Drake's cases involved.

The professor chuckled. "Your father certainly did make some unusual requests over the years, but then again, there was a reason he had a … certain reputation. I have it on good authority you've followed in his footsteps."

Penelope's face turned red. "You could say that."

Professor Boyd was a folklorist, specializing in the folklore of the American South. Judging by the small arsenal at her disposal, as well as the titles of the books on the shelf behind her desk, she was well prepared for anything Penelope's father could have thrown at her.

"So, what strange question can I answer for you today?" she asked.

Penelope glanced at Zed. "We're looking for a graveyard near Columbia, probably one for black families, possibly abandoned. I know it's not a lot to go on, but there might be a sign or something with the word *happiness* on it. You wouldn't know about such a place, would you?"

Professor Boyd scrunched her nose and tilted her head, then stood and pulled a book down from her bookshelf. "Are you planning on going legend tripping?"

Penelope frowned. "Legend tripping?"

"A visit to a place where some tragic, horrific, or supernatural event supposedly happened," Zed said, "usually at night, usually by a group of young people wanting to get all hot and bothered."

Penelope twisted her mouth into a wry grin. "You mean like college students."

"Exactly. You don't want to know the number of students who've gotten in trouble for trespassing over the years." The professor opened the book and began thumbing through it. "Graveyards especially. Seems it never occurs to anyone that most cemeteries are on private property."

Penelope leaned forward, craning her neck for a better look at the book. "So, you think you know where this grave-yard is?"

Professor Boyd nodded and pointed to a picture in the book. A wrought-iron sign half covered in vines stood above a broken gate. It said, "Happiness Community Cemetery." Zed stiffened and hoped the professor didn't see his reaction.

"Happiness was the name of a community founded by freed slaves after the end of the Civil War," she explained. "It's abandoned now, and it's hard to find, on purpose. For decades there have been ghost sightings in the area, but they bulldozed over the road leading to the community after a number of serious accidents put some curious legend trip-pers in the hospital."

"Why was it abandoned?" asked Penelope.

"A curse if the stories are to be believed," replied Professor Boyd. "One of the members of the community was a root worker originally from the Sea Islands just below Charleston. According to the stories, her daughter was assaulted and killed. She accused one of her neighbor's sons, but the neighbor was well-liked, so no one believed her. So, on a night without any moon, she took justice into her own hands. She walked into the center of the graveyard and cursed them all, sealing the hex with her own blood."

Zed grunted. "A blood curse. That's serious. I'm afraid to

ask what it was."

The professor eyed Zed again, suspicious, and curious. "She declared no one in Happiness would ever find their rest as long as her daughter's killer went unpunished. And they didn't. Anytime someone died, their ghost came back to haunt their living relatives. The more people died, the more ghosts, until the town became uninhabitable. Everyone who could, moved away. After the last resident died, nature reclaimed Happiness. A lot of the buildings are still there, but they're falling apart. That's how people get hurt, going into places that aren't safe. Of course, afterward they say something lured them in, or pushed them, or tripped them."

There were other photographs, of the cemetery, of some of the falling-down buildings, including a church. If Zed wasn't mistaken, someone stood in the doorway of the church, though the front of the building was in shadow, and it was hard to tell. The figure was only halfway there—if there at all—fading out just below the waist.

Penelope caught her breath. She saw it, too. "If, hypothetically, one were to want to visit Happiness, how would one get there?"

"It's just north of the city, off Highway 321, near the intersection with Cedar Creek Road. Like I said, it's hard to find, but you should still be able to see the remnants of the old road if you look hard enough."

"Thank you. That helps a lot." Penelope stood. "I'm sure you're busy. We won't keep you any longer."

"You're very welcome. I'm glad to help. Any time." Professor Boyd closed the book and put it back in its place on the shelf. "If, hypothetically, one were to go looking for Happiness, though, I'd recommend waiting until tomorrow. If you leave now you won't get there until after sunset, and it's easy to get lost in the dark."

Zed nodded. "We'll be sure to heed that advice. Hypothetically."

Penelope threw him a sidelong glance. She probably would have elbowed him if the professor hadn't held up a hand.

"Wait, one more thing before you go."

Penelope turned her attention back to Professor Boyd. "What is it?"

"It's interesting you should stop by now. I had a visit from a police detective yesterday. He wanted to know about some of the cases I helped your father with while he was on the police force."

Penelope glanced at Zed again, this time with a wary look. "Really? What did you tell him?"

The professor shrugged. "I told him what I remembered. I mostly helped your father build criminal profiles. Even though I'm not a psychologist, a great deal of my work is based on how people think about the world around them. He seemed satisfied with that answer. He politely thanked me for my time, and then left." She scanned her desk and picked up a card. "Here, he gave me his card."

Zed read it over Penelope's shoulder.

Detective James Everett

"What's Detective Everett doing asking questions about your father's old cases?" Zed asked once they were back in Penelope's Lincoln.

"I don't know," Penelope replied as she started up the car and threw it in reverse, "but we can't deal with that right now. We've got other things to worry about."

"True. This graveyard sounds like a perfect place to sum-

summon a high-level demon. The boundary has to be pretty thin there, what with all the ghosts."

"If you believe the stories."

Zed looked at Penelope in surprise. "You don't?"

"Sometimes stories are just stories, Zed."

"You saw the ghost in the picture, too, Penelope."

"But that still doesn't mean the story Professor Boyd told was true."

"There has to be a reason your father and Ephraim went there in the first place."

Penelope gripped the steering wheel until her knuckles turned white. "I know that."

"Then what's the problem?" Zed persisted.

Penelope sighed and let her shoulders slump. "Do you honestly think my father would actually go along with a plan to summon a demon? I won't believe it, even if he was young and reckless."

There it was. That was the reason the visit to Professor Boyd had her so upset.

"There's another possibility you might consider," Zed prodded gently.

"What would that be?" She wasn't bothering to hide the annoyance in her voice.

"Maybe he was only pretending to go along with it. Maybe he knew how dangerous it was to be summoning a demon like that, and he went there that night to stop it."

She snorted. "That's insane. He could have gotten himself killed."

Zed wagged a finger at her. "Hey, you're the one who called him reckless."

The rest of the trip back to Penelope's office passed in silence. Zed watched outside the window as they traced their way through neighborhoods with tree-lined streets, past cozy little houses where no one worried about ghosts or demons or failing to protect the people they loved.

"Can you let Bertram know we're taking a road trip?" Penelope asked when they pulled up in front of the old converted house that served as her home and her office. "I'm going to go talk to Charles. Regroup here in an hour?"

Zed frowned. "What about what Professor Boyd said? About waiting until tomorrow?"

Penelope shook her head. "We can't afford to do that. We don't know how much time Ephraim has left, if it isn't already too late."

Zed studied her profile. Penelope was right, of course. The longer Ephraim Brown went missing, the less of a chance they had of finding him alive, but Zed could see another motive written in her tensed jaw and also hear it in her strained voice. She was desperate to find out what happened to her father, and she'd do just about anything to get to the truth.

Charles turned another card over. By now he imagined the grinning man who stared back at him from the card's face was mocking him. He'd performed close to a dozen readings, using three different decks, but every time, the Nine of Cups—the Lord of Happiness—turned up. The odds of that happening by chance were close to zero.

What the card foretold, Charles had no idea, but he knew for damn sure it didn't mean he could expect any happy news in his future.

He shuffled the deck again for another reading, but before he could turn any more cards over, he heard a noise from behind the house. He glanced out the window, his gaze going immediately to the place where they had buried Patrick

Wheeler, near the tree line about fifty yards from the back door.

It was the best they could do at the time, though Charles wasn't thrilled with the idea of making his back yard into a private cemetery for dark magicians. Patrick wasn't coming back—not in body and not in spirit. He had made sure of that. Still, the shadows around the burial place seemed a little bit darker than they should have been, taking the shape of a man covered in a burial shroud. He blinked, and the illusion was gone.

Charles turned his attention to the damaged book on his work table. He took a deep breath in an effort to slow his racing heartbeat. No more Patrick Wheeler. No more Brown family. No more Lord of Happiness. No more Shrouded Man. He wanted to lose himself in the work of repairing the old book. It was the only time he ever found any peace.

He turned up the radio before he sat down. Instead of the soulful sounds of Mahalia Jackson or another gospel singer, though, Dizzy Gillespie's trumpet blared from the speakers as Charles picked up his X-acto knife.

A knock on the back door immediately derailed his plans. Swearing under his breath, he went to answer and swung open the door to reveal Penelope standing on his back steps.

"Hi, Charles," she said. "You busy?"

Charles glanced back over his shoulder at his work table and the half-dismantled book lying among his tools. "A little."

Penelope chewed on her lower lip. "Sorry, but this is kind of important. Can I come in?"

Sighing, Charles stepped aside.

"I knocked on the front door, but you didn't answer," Penelope said as she entered. "I heard music coming from around the back of the house, so I figured you'd be back here." She pointed to the radio. "That's not Mahalia Jackson."

"No, it isn't."

She narrowed her eyes. "It's just, you don't normally listen to—"

"Don't assume you know everything about me," Charles snapped. "You said it was important. What's going on?"

A hurt expression crossed her face, but vanished as quickly as it appeared. "Ephraim Brown is missing. He disappeared two days ago."

"You want me to help find him? You got a lock of his hair for me?"

"Actually, we think we know where he is. Have you ever heard of a place called Happiness?"

Charles' blood froze. "Is that supposed to be a joke?"

"No, it's a real place. Or it used to be. It's an abandoned community near Columbia, founded by freed slaves." She waved a hand. "It's really a long story. I can explain all of it on the way."

Charles crossed his arms. His feet remained where they were. "Who says I'm going anywhere?"

Penelope frowned. "We need you, Charles."

"You always need me."

She pursed her lips. "Look, I get it. We've asked a lot of you lately, more than we probably should have. But we don't have a prayer of stopping whatever is going on without you."

"You don't have a prayer of stopping it with me either."

"What are you saying?"

"I'm saying I don't have the first clue about that pentagram you gave me, and I'm not going to miraculously find the answer in one of my books this time. If I don't know what it is, I don't know how to stop it. In all likelihood, Ephraim Brown is dead. Let him go."

"What if it doesn't stop with him?" she asked.

"Let them all go, the whole Brown family."

She shook her head. "They don't deserve that."

Charles stifled a laugh. "Don't they? Are they really worth sacrificing yourself, Penelope?"

"This isn't like you, Charles, to not care." Her voice trembled in frustrated anger.

"I have cared, Penelope, more than you know," he said, "but did you ever stop to think that maybe the Browns brought this on themselves? My ... Margaret heard stories about them."

"But what if this goes beyond the Browns? What do we do then?"

"Find a hole to hide in," he replied.

She glared. "Fine. Do what you want. Zed and I are going regardless. We're not just going to stand by and let any more innocent people die."

"There you go using that word again."

Penelope spun on her heels to leave without saying anything else. Charles glanced down at the deck of tarot cards resting on the edge of his work table. As he watched, the entire deck skewed sideways until the top card tipped over and fell to the floor, landing face up. Once again, the Lord of Happiness leered up at Charles with his mocking grin.

"Wait," Charles called after Penelope, who paused with her hand on the doorknob to the back door. "I need to take care of some things first. You go on. I'll meet you at your place in a little bit."

Penelope smiled. "Don't be too long."

When Penelope arrived back at her house, she noted, with no small amount of annoyance, that she'd beaten Zed and

Bertram there. She thought for sure they'd be there already. They'd wasted so much time.

Time they didn't have to begin with.

Time they needed to save Ephraim.

Time she could have used to find out the truth about her father.

As she climbed the steps to the porch a sickly-sweet smell assaulted her nose, like flowers beginning to die, but it was almost November, and the flowers were long gone. She had just put her housekey in the door when the shadow fell over it. A rough hand reached around and covered her mouth with a wet handkerchief. The sickly-sweet smell filled her nostrils.

"Don't try to struggle," he growled.

But she couldn't struggle even if she wanted to. He was bigger than she was, and his arms held her like a vise. She recognized his voice from the threatening phone call she'd gotten a few months back, after a gold Ford tried to run her car off the road and someone threw a brick through her window. She wondered briefly if this was the same man she'd caught staring at her at church the day she'd visited her grandmother, but she didn't have much time to consider the possibility. Her head became fuzzy. It got harder and harder to think. Black dots formed at the edges of her vision, multiplying and growing until everything went dark.

Zed didn't see Bertram's red Camaro in front of his apartment building when he pulled up. That was going to put a kink in Penelope's plans. Bertram hadn't told Zed he was going out. Then again, Bertram was a grown man and didn't need Zed's permission to leave the apartment.

When Zed walked through his front door, he didn't find

the apartment empty, though. Jake sat on his sofa, next to the pillow and folded-up blanket Bertram had been using to crash there.

"Jake?" Zed said. "How did you get in?"

"Through the door," Jake replied.

"Through the *locked* door? Don't tell me Bertram left it unlocked. I mean, granted he's had a lot on his mind, but I did give him a key."

"Bertram? Is that his name?" Jake pointed to the pillow and blanket on the sofa. "Is that who's been staying here with you?"

Zed didn't like the strange tone in Jake's voice. "Well, yeah. I'm just letting him crash here for a few days. He's … uh … going through some things."

"Are you sure that's all there is?"

"What more would there be?"

Jake stood. "What are you hiding, Zed? Why didn't you tell me?"

"What? You mean you think me and Bertram … Oh, trust me that would never happen, for so, so many reasons. What's wrong, Jake? Are you okay?"

"I'm fine," he replied, just a little too calmly.

Zed saw the flash of metal in Jake's hand almost too late. The knife came inches from slashing Zed's throat, but fortunately he was faster than Jake and sidestepped the attack. Jake spun around to face him again, clumsily lunging with the knife.

Zed did his best to stay out of reach in the small room. "Jake, what the fuck do you think you're doing?"

Jake didn't reply. He instead hurled himself at Zed again. Zed dodged the knife blade, pushing off of Jake and sending him headlong into the wall. Jake let out an animal cry of frustration.

"What's wrong with you? Stop! I don't want to hurt you."

While backing up, Zed stumbled over his recliner. Jake pounced on top of him, bringing the knife down in a deadly arc. Zed clutched Jake's forearm with both hands, stopping the knife's descent, but Jake was strong, stronger than he should have been. An unnatural green light flashed in his eyes, and for just a moment his shadow moved slightly out of sync with the rest of him.

A daemon. Jake was possessed by a daemon.

"Get out!" Zed screamed. "Get out of him now."

He threw all the willpower he could into the charm bracelet Charles had made for him and tried to channel some of his own magic as well, raw though it was. Blue and violet energy crackled around his arm, and the next thing he knew, Jake went flying backward across the room. He hit the wall and dropped the knife from his hand. Jake's body slumped to the floor while a dark, shadowy form rose up, taking up most of the space in the room, making it hard for Zed to breathe.

Two green points of light fixed on him, their malice impossible to escape, but Zed stood his ground. He held his arm up in front of his face, the charm bracelet encircling his wrist still sparking. He recited the Lord's Prayer and the Twenty-third Psalm and the *Vade Retro Satana* at the top of his lungs. The thing shrieked and moaned, but when Zed lowered his arm again, it was gone.

Zed rushed over to Jake, relieved to find him still breathing. Zed tried to rouse him. Jake groaned and his eyes fluttered, but Zed couldn't wake him up. He took the charm bracelet off his wrist and put it on Jake's.

Still nothing.

Zed paced the floor for a couple of minutes trying to figure out what to do. There was no way he was going to take Jake along with them to find Happiness, not if the visions were true and they were all headed into a forest teeming with daemons. Zed would never forgive himself if anything happened to Jake.

But he also couldn't leave Jake alone in the state he was in. Who to leave him with was the problem. Jake had never exactly introduced him to any family or friends, not that Zed really blamed him. Their relationship could easily put both of them in harm's way, as Jake had reminded him. And then it dawned on him that he *did* know a few of Jake's friends. He picked up the phone and dialed the Greenville headquarters of McGovern for President.

"Hi, Linda, thank God you're the one who answered the phone," he said. "This is Zed McKay. We met yesterday. I'm Jake's friend. Listen, Jake's … sick, and I need someone to look after him. I can't do it because I have to go out of town. Last minute trip. Dealing with an emergency of my own. … No, no, he doesn't need to go to the hospital. He just needs someone to stay with him until he sleeps it off. … Thanks, Linda, you're a lifesaver. Let me give you my address."

When Penelope opened her eyes, she found herself in a dark room. A thin line of light traced the edges of heavy curtains drawn over a large window. The bright white sliver was just enough for Penelope to make out the other shapes in the room. A bed. A desk. A dresser. A television.

She was in a motel somewhere.

One by one, her other senses returned. The muffled sounds of a television vibrated through the wall from the next room over, the smell of stale cigarettes and musky cologne assaulted her nose, and a dull ache rose from her arms and legs. She tried to stand, but found she couldn't. Only then did she realize she was tied to a chair, with her wrists bound together behind her back. Someone had ripped up the bed sheets to use as rope.

Fortunately, she still had some range of motion in her arms, just enough to work at the knots at her wrists. Her father had insisted on teaching her a number of useful life skills, like how to change a flat tire, how to make a deposit at the bank, how to pick a lock with a hairpin, and how to get out of being tied up. It took about twenty minutes to work one of the knots halfway free, but she stopped when a metallic click drew her attention to the motel room door. Someone put a key in the lock.

The door opened, and light flooded into the room, blinding Penelope for a moment. When her eyes adjusted, she saw an older man with black, thinning hair standing in the doorway. In his hand he held a brown paper bag. He wore a flannel shirt and a pair of jeans, and at least a day's worth of stubble covered his face, but he glared at her the same way he had that Sunday when she met his gaze from across the church sanctuary. Then, he was clean-shaven and in a three-piece suit. She couldn't say she was surprised. If she had to guess, he'd left a gold Ford parked just outside.

When he saw her, his lips spread in an unpleasant smile. "Oh, good. You're up."

"Who are you?" Penelope asked, continuing to work at the knots around her wrists.

He feigned a hurt expression as he shut the door, plunging the room into near darkness again. "You know who I am, Miss Drake. You and your little lackey took enough pictures of me, and then you handed them over to that bitch."

Of course. How could she forget? "Ronald Gaines."

He turned on a lamp. The nasty grin returned, even more unsettling with his features thrown into sharp relief by the lamplight. "That's me."

Penelope had been hired by his wife Joyce to spy on him because she suspected he was seeing another woman. As it turned out, Mrs. Gaines was right.

His mouth curled into a snarl. "She took away everything I had because of you. I lost my house. I lost all my money. My kids won't look me in the eye. My former friends cross the street to avoid me. You destroyed my life."

She refused to look away as he leered at her. "I think maybe you did that when you decided to have an affair."

He spun around and raised his arm. Penelope braced herself for the back of his hand across her face, but the blow never came.

"You don't know anything about me," he yelled, angry tears welling in his eyes. "You don't know anything about my life. All you did was sit across the street and take pictures of something that was none of your business. Who are you to pass judgment on me?"

"I was just doing my job," she said quietly.

"No, you don't get to use that excuse." He set the bag he had brought with him on the desk next to the door and pulled out a gun. "I'm going to make sure you pay for what you've done."

He retrieved the magazine from the bag. His hands shook as he tried to load it into the gun, and it took him several attempts. It was obvious to Penelope he'd never held a firearm before.

She just needed to keep him talking.

"You don't have to do this."

"What choice do I have?" he asked as he looked down at the loaded gun in his hand.

"Seems to me you've got a lot of choices. You could try to put your life back together."

He let out a dry, bitter laugh. "Why? I'm a middle-aged

insurance salesman. Some life there. I come home from work, heat up a TV dinner, and fall asleep to the eleven o'clock news. Then the next day I get up and do it all over again."

Just a little bit longer. "You can't possibly think you'll get away with it. You're not even wearing gloves. And you don't have a silencer. Everyone will hear the gunshot."

"Who said anything about getting away? This is going to be all over the news for months. Every time she turns on the television, she's going to have to deal with me."

The last knot slipped from her wrists, and suddenly Penelope's hands were free. For the time being, though, she held the makeshift rope behind her back.

"Now it's not going to do any good for you to try to spoil things," he continued. "No more talking for you."

He put the gun down and picked up the ruined bedsheet, which lay in a heap on the floor at the foot of the bed. He tore off another strip and came toward her, but as soon as he leaned down to tie it over her mouth, she grabbed his arm with both hands and bit down as hard as she could, enough to break the skin. He shrieked and jerked away.

"What the hell is wrong with you?" he screamed as he surveyed the bloody set of teeth marks on his forearm.

She shook her head. "Nothing. I'm just trying not to get shot."

She really didn't have much of a plan, though. Her legs were still tied to the chair, and she didn't think she could un-tie herself before Gaines reached the gun. So, she did the only thing she could think to do. She pitched forward onto her feet and threw herself at him, chair and all. Together, they toppled to the floor, knocking the lamp off the desk. The lightbulb shattered with a pop, and the darkness returned. Her weight combined with the chair pinned Gaines to the ground while she struggled to work her legs free.

"Get off me, you crazy bitch!" Gaines yelled.

He flailed his arms and legs until he managed to shove her off. He scrambled up from the floor and made a reach for the gun, but Penelope hooked an arm around his leg, and he went down hard, banging his head against the desk. While he was still dazed, she slipped out of the knots around her ankles, and before he could get back to his feet, she slammed the chair down on top of him. Then she dashed for the door. She threw it open and ran out into the dazzling light of the motel parking lot. She had no idea where she was, but she didn't stop.

She was halfway across the parking lot when the gunshot rang out. She threw herself to the ground, expecting another, but no second shot came. She glanced back over her shoulder. Ronald Gaines leaned against the frame of the open motel room door. A giant red hole marred one temple. The gun fell from his hand, and he crumpled to the ground.

Penelope jumped to her feet and kept running.

Zed was still standing outside his apartment building when Bertram's Camaro pulled up. He had just seen Linda off with a still half-conscious Jake stuffed into the passenger seat of her VW. She'd given them both a lot of odd looks, especially after Jake started mumbling in something that sounded like Latin, but she promised she'd take Jake back to his apartment and stay with him there. The charm bracelet would keep them safe, Zed hoped.

"Everything okay?" Bertram asked as he climbed out of his car.

"Not exactly," Zed replied. "Where were you?"

"I was just driving around, doing some thinking, trying to

clear my head." Bertram glanced down at his shoes. He wanted to say more, Zed could tell. He was just looking for the words. "Those books, you said Bobby Parker's sister left them with you? I was looking through some of them. They … look a lot like books my dad has. I never knew what they really were. It's just a weird place to be in, you know, having to rethink your whole life."

Zed knew exactly what he was talking about.

Bertram sighed. "So, anyway, what did I miss?"

Zed pasted on a crooked grin. "Where do I start? For one, we're going on a road trip."

Penelope didn't answer the door when Zed and Bertram finally made it to her house, even though her car was parked outside.

"Maybe she's gone somewhere with Charles to get something he thinks we might need," Bertram said.

Zed shot him a dubious look. "You don't really believe that."

Bertram shook his head. "No, I don't."

About that time Charles pulled up in his wreck of a truck. Alone. Now Zed knew something was really wrong. He and Bertram waited for Charles to join them on the porch.

"She left my place a couple of hours ago," Charles said after they told him Penelope wasn't answering the door.

"Why didn't you come back with her?" Zed asked, his tone a little more accusatory than he intended.

"I had some things to take care of," Charles replied with ice in his voice.

Zed put his hands on his hips. "Well, where the hell is she?"

Bertram stared at the door. "She could be in there, unable

to answer."

Zed and Charles looked at him, and then each other.

"Only one way to find out, I guess." Zed backed up, preparing to kick the door in.

Before he could, though, someone called his name. They all turned to see a black and yellow checked taxi parked in front of the house. Penelope was climbing out of the back seat. The look on her face told him something really wasn't right.

Zed rushed down the steps and over to her. "Penelope, what happened?"

She didn't say anything. She just collapsed against him, wrapping her arms around his midsection and burying her face in his chest. He hugged her as her whole body convulsed in sobs.

"What happened, Penelope?" he repeated.

She still didn't answer, so he stood, quietly embracing her, until she stopped crying. Finally, she took a deep breath and let go of him, reaching up to wipe the tears away from her cheeks. "I'll tell you on the way." She looked over her shoulder at the taxi, still waiting. "Could … could you pay the cab driver? I don't have my purse."

Zed was going to argue with her about leaving right then, about how they could wait until the morning to confront whatever was waiting for them in Happiness, South Carolina, but he couldn't. They were out of time. They had to go. They had to deal with it, for Ephraim, for Jake, for all of them. He reached into his back pocket for his wallet.

When Ephraim opened his eyes, he was ten years old again, hiding underneath the dining room table in his grandparents' house. Everything was quiet, except for the ticking of the grandfather clock in the entryway. He didn't know why he was hiding, alone in the darkened house, only that he needed to. He hugged his knees and tried to push down the rising panic, but that was a losing battle.

Suddenly the grandfather clock rang out the hour. The shadows grew darker, and from inside the walls came sounds of scratching and shuffling, as if something was trying to break through. The front door opened, and heavy boots made the hardwood floors shake. Ephraim scrambled out from under the table between the chairs and ran upstairs to his grandparents' bedroom.

A giant four-poster bed dominated the center of the room. He ducked behind it, up against the wall, away from the door, but there was no use trying to hide. The door opened. Ephraim put his hands over his head in an effort to get as small as he could, but a rough hand grabbed him by his shirt collar and yanked him up. Soon he was looking into the angry face of his father.

"Boy, what are you doing up here?" he snarled. "You know you can't hide from me."

Before Ephraim could answer, the scene dissolved. His father, the four-poster bed, the house, it all vanished, replaced by overgrown gravestones in the middle of the woods and the sounds of the night.

Ephraim remembered. All of it.

He sat cross-legged on the cold ground. Jonathan Drake sat to his left, Geoffrey Wheeler to his right. Torchlight threw dancing shadows over the faces of Bradley James and Edward McDowall who sat facing him. Together the five of them formed a circle, or—although it didn't occur to Ephraim at the time—the points of a star. Jude Hall, the sixth member of their delinquent band, stood in the center, holding the torch.

They had trekked through the woods to the abandoned graveyard for a ritual, an initiation. If they got caught sneaking out of their dormitory, they'd all get expelled, but it would be worth the risk if everything went well that night— or so Ephraim and the others had been told. Pass the test, and everything they ever wanted would be theirs.

Except it was all a lie.

Jonathan figured out the truth. Ephraim's first instinct when Jonathan told him was to back out and refuse to go, but Jonathan argued they'd just find others to take their places. He convinced Ephraim they had to go along so they could stop the ritual. Now Ephraim was rethinking that plan.

Jude held the torch high over his head and began to chant. On the ground around his feet glowing lines flared to life, radiating outward toward each of them, connecting them all in a giant pentagram. Strange symbols wove around the lines. They hurt to look at. Ephraim and Jonathan played along when the others let out muted gasps and traded nervous glances. No one dared move from their spot, though.

Jude's chanting grew louder, and the dark figures Ephraim had seen before emerged from behind the gravestones. Made of pure darkness, they oozed their way toward the pentagram, until they formed a wall of shadows around the group. Genuine panic spread around the circle, but still none of them moved. It was all part of the test surely. If they got up and ran, they failed.

A giant raven landed next to Jude, bigger than any Ephraim had ever seen. Silently, it walked around the circle staring at each of them in turn. When it turned one beady, black eye toward Ephraim, he felt all his secrets laid bare. The black disc of its eye grew, expanding until the empty nothingness blotted out the firelight. It drew Ephraim in, enticing him to come closer, to reach out to it and be lost forever. No more worries. No more cares. No more pain. Just … nothing.

The giant bird cawed, and Ephraim blinked, the illusion shattered. The raven spread its wings, and with a single flap, it perched on Jude's shoulder. He didn't even seem to notice. His eyes were closed. His mouth still moved, but his words were barely audible.

Ephraim glanced at Jonathan, who gave a subtle nod. Ephraim removed a rosary from his pocket. A silver cross dangled from the string of beads.

"*Vade retro, Satana,*" he cried.

Step back, Satan.

Ephraim's performance was mostly a distraction, though. They needed something a little more primeval than a Latin rite to stop Jude. While Ephraim continued to recite the Prayer of Saint Benedict, Jonathan took out a pocket knife. He slashed the palm of his hand and made a fist, squeezing until the blood seeped through his fingers.

As soon as the drops of blood touched the ground, the whole forest screamed. The wind whipped up around them and blew out the torch in Jude's hand. The black shapes that had been standing sentry wailed and moaned and lashed out with clawed hands, tentacles and mouths full of sharp teeth, but they stopped short of crossing the pentagram's perimeter.

Jude had stopped chanting. Instead, he stood facing Ephraim and Jonathan, his hair wild, his face contorted in rage. In that moment, the giant raven swooped down on Ephraim, knocking him to the ground. It tried to rip the rosary out of his hand with its claws while it pecked at his face with its beak.

Jonathan attacked the bird, stabbing it with his knife. The raven squawked and flew off. Ephraim struggled to sit up.

Scratches covered his hands. Something wet and warm ran into his left eye. It stung.

Jonathan turned toward Jude. "Banish the demon back to where it came from."

"You don't have any idea what you're doing," Jude snarled. "You could have had anything you wanted."

Jonathan held out his bloody hand. "Not this way. Banish the demon, or I will."

Jude glared. "You don't know how."

He resumed his chanting. The lines of the pentagram glowed anew, and the shadow demons went back to their vigil at the pentagram's edges. At the same time, new words tumbled out of Jonathan's mouth, the same as those Jude recited, but in a different order, like a song sung in a round. It seemed as if they were going to settle into a prolonged duel, until Jonathan threw his knife at Jude. It pinwheeled through the air, and the blade stuck in Jude's arm. Jude cried out. With an infuriated roar, he pulled the knife out of his arm and tossed it aside, but he'd lost the rhythm of the incantation.

Jonathan's words overpowered him. Jude clutched the sides of his head and screamed for Jonathan to stop, but Jonathan continued, a look of determination on his face. The wind picked up again, and the shadows screeched, fleeing back to wherever they had come from. Somewhere above, the lonely call of a raven echoed.

When Jonathan stopped and the wind died, Jude lay in the middle of the broken pentagram, alive but unmoving. The others had all run away. Ephraim wanted to leave Jude there, but Jonathan said they couldn't do that. He had been their friend once. Maybe he wasn't completely responsible for his actions that night. And so they picked him up and carried him through the woods, back toward civilization.

In the days that followed, Ephraim couldn't get the raven out of his head. It spoke to him in a hoarse voice all day and all night, drowning out nearly every other thought, beckoning him to return to the darkness, to embrace the nothingness.

It would all be over.

It wouldn't hurt anymore.

When he couldn't stand the voice any longer, he told Jonathan, and Jonathan … did something to make him forget. Ever since, Ephraim had only a vague idea of what happened that night. Jonathan told him he'd just gotten drunk.

When Ephraim's eyes opened for the final time, he was still in the cemetery. He couldn't move. He could barely even feel his arms and legs. He looked up to see the branches of a tree rising above him and the coils of rope around his outstretched arms. The same rope bound his legs to the tree as well. The bark scoured his back. His mouth was dry, and his lungs were on fire. He had no idea how much time had passed.

Something stirred in the underbrush at the edge of the clearing. Ephraim barely had enough energy to turn his head. A man emerged from the trees, long gray hair in tangled knots and pale blue eyes crazed. Nearly forty years had passed, but Ephraim recognized him right away.

Jude Hall.

He rushed toward Ephraim, the blade of the knife he held gleaming in the moonlight. Ephraim could only watch as he swung his arm in a wide arc and slashed open Ephraim's throat. As the warm blood spilled out of the gash, and with it, Ephraim's life, a smile spread across his face. At least he had remembered.

Bertram woke with a start. He glanced around. He was in the back seat of Penelope's Lincoln. Charles sat next to him, cradling his leather satchel in his lap. Penelope sat in the front on the passenger's side. Zed drove.

"What … what happened?"

"Nothing," Charles said. "You dozed off."

Bertram glanced out the car window, but it was too dark to see anything. "Where are we?"

"We just passed Chapin," Zed answered. "Almost there."

"That is, if we can even find this place," Charles added.

"We have to find it," Penelope said. "We don't have a choice."

"I think I might be able to help with that." Bertram stared back at three pairs of skeptical eyes. "What? I'm not allowed to have weird dreams, too?"

Charles glanced sideways at Bertram. He'd been adamant when he told Zed to pull over, pointing to a patch of darkness by the side of the road. To Charles, it was indistinguishable from all the other patches of darkness they'd passed by in the last half hour, but Bertram insisted it was the old road to Happiness.

Zed parked the car as far off the road as he could, and they all climbed out. Each of them had a flashlight. Zed shined his into the woods. Sure enough, there was a gap in the trees, easy to overlook, but plain to see if you knew what you were looking for.

Dry leaves crunched under their feet as they made their way single-file through the forest. Zed took the lead. Charles brought up the rear. None of them had much to say. Even Zed was uncharacteristically quiet, for which Charles was grateful.

A few dozen yards from the road, the path widened and flattened out. Before too long, they came to the stone foundations of long-gone buildings, and beyond that a few structures with walls still intact, though overgrown with vegetation.

It would have been easy for Charles to imagine things in those half-collapsed buildings watching them, waiting for them, but Charles knew better. He didn't have to imagine. They were there. All the ghosts of the people of Happiness, doomed never to find rest.

Soon voices came to his ears, people talking, not in hushed whispers as he might have expected, but loud, boisterous conversations. They seemed to come from every direction. Then the music started, low at first but gradually getting louder. None of the others seemed to hear anything. As Charles looked around for the source of the noise, a flash of blue in the woods caught his eye. And then another.

Out of nowhere a trumpet blared. The strings of a bass thrummed, and a piano set down a staccato rhythm. Charles recognized the tune. It was a favorite of the jazz trio from the Blue Club. With his next step, Charles walked out of the woods near Columbia, South Carolina, in 1972 and back in time more than fifty years, into Isaiah Jenkins' Harlem.

The Blue Club was hopping. Every table was full, and so was the dance floor. But no one was there for the Bill Porter Three, as good as they were. When they finished their set, a hush fell over the room as Millie Priest took the stage, stunning as ever. From the very first note she sang, she owned the place.

Charles smiled as Isaiah's memories of the months since he'd been gone filled in—lazy mornings huddled under warm blankets in bed, walks in the new-fallen snow, nights in Millie's dressing room after the club closed. There seemed to be fewer of those, though. Despite Prohibition, the Blue Club was busier than ever, and it wasn't uncommon for Charles to be busy until three or four in the morning after a packed night.

Of course, the reason for that was the speakeasy in the basement selling bootleg liquor. Charles had been cut out of that part of the business, but he knew all too well about it, especially the number of times Millie disappeared down there for private performances.

His eyes fell on Andre Lestrade at the best table in the place, watching Millie sing. Charles didn't like the smile on his face. He wasn't just enjoying Millie's beautiful voice. His grin was possessive, as if he were enjoying something from a collection he owned.

And Millie's gaze, more times than not, was on him. Charles knew she was just putting on a show, but it still bothered him.

After her set, she returned backstage. By then Andre was gone from his seat, too. On an impulse, Charles decided he needed to check on Millie. He went to her dressing room, but she didn't answer when he knocked on her door.

He went to the speakeasy next. There was a hidden door just past the stage, out of sight from the rest of the room. A secret knock and a password let special patrons in. The password changed weekly, as did the knock. Charles rapped on the door with his knuckles—three quick taps, a pause, and then another tap.

When the door cracked open, Charles whispered the password. "Azure."

The bouncer, the same one who had tried to stop Charles from seeing Millie in her dressing room on his first night at the club, let him through. A short flight of stairs led to another door and another bouncer. He opened the door for Charles, who stepped inside. This room wasn't any less packed than the room upstairs. A piano player in the corner hammered out an upbeat tune, and cigar smoke hung heavy in the air. Here, the bar was fully stocked, and the liquor flowed. Charles scanned the room. He found Millie quickly, seated at a table with Andre and his entourage. He had his arm around her. She was laughing at something someone said.

When they made eye contact across the room, though, her smile faded. She turned to Andre and whispered something in his ear. He nodded, and she stood up. She circled the room before approaching him, speaking with some of the other patrons along the way. When she reached him, she grabbed him by the arm and pulled him aside.

"What are you doing here?" she asked.

"I could ask you the same question," he snapped.

She crossed her arms. "I'm working."

Charles glanced at her empty seat at Andre's table. "Doesn't seem like you're doing any singing right now."

"That's not all of my job."

"Really? That's news to me."

Millie ran her fingers down his arm. It was as much of a display of affection as they risked, but her touch still made him tingle. "Listen, we can talk about this later. I need to get back."

He cocked an eyebrow. "And do what?"

"Andre likes me to sit with him when we have VIPs. He says it makes the room more attractive." She added in a low voice, "Nothing has happened, and nothing is going to happen."

Charles didn't get a chance to say anything else. The door

flew open, and the body of the bouncer fell into the room. Over it leapt three men, all with guns drawn. They immediately started firing.

The gunshots sent the room into chaos. People shouted, trying to get out or dive for cover somewhere. The bullets missed Andre, but one of his men when sprawling across the table, an angry red bloom on his forehead. The bullets would have hit Millie had she been sitting next to him. Andre's men had their guns drawn now too, and they were returning fire.

Charles pulled Millie down behind the bar. His stomach turned in knots as he remembered the date. March 18. The day Millie was supposed to be shot and killed.

He looked at her, panic on her face as they crouched down. He had saved her before. Maybe he had just saved her again. Maybe that's why he was there.

"Can we get to the other door?" he asked as bullets shattered the glasses above the bar.

"What other door?"

Charles risked a glance around the side of the bar but ducked back when a bullet splintered off a chunk of it just next to his head. "You and I know full well there's another door for situations just like this. I'm sure Andre's used it already."

Millie shook her head. "It's clear across the room. I don't know if we can make it."

"We've got to find a way."

As he peered around the bar again, his training from Vietnam came back to him. He noted where all the shooters were. He could see a pathway through the chairs and tables. They could make it if they kept moving.

He took her hand. "Come this way. I think I can get us out of here."

She hesitated. "Are you sure?"

"Yes, just trust me. I can do it." Charles looked in time to see another one of Andre's men go down. "Come on. Let's go."

Millie pulled her hand back. "Wait, Charles."

He looked at her. "What did you call me?"

"I called you by your name."

"You called me Charles. I'm Isaiah."

She didn't say anything.

It was as if all the color drained from Charles' vision. "None of this is real."

"But it can be." Millie offered him her hand again. "We can leave here. Find somewhere else to go. Maybe Chicago. We can be together."

He shook his head. "No, it still won't be real. This has all been a set-up, in case I got hold of those books, to keep me busy, distracted."

Her expression hardened. "You don't have to do this."

"Yes, I do." He kissed her on the forehead and wiped a tear from her cheek. "I love you, Millie Priest. I've enjoyed our time together more than you will ever know, but I have other people who need me."

He stood up over the bar, and not a second later he caught a bullet in his chest. The pain was more than anything he ever imagined. As he fell backward, Millie screamed.

Charles woke up staring at the night sky.

"Hey, I think he's awake," someone said.

Suddenly Penelope's face appeared in his field of vision.

"Charles? Are you okay?" she asked.

He managed to push himself up into a sitting position. His head pounded. "Yeah, I think so."

Penelope crouched down beside him. "What happened?"

"I'd rather not talk about it." Penelope opened her mouth to protest, but he held up a hand. "Someday, I promise. Right now, I think we've got bigger problems. Where is this cemetery?"

Bertram offered him a hand in getting to his feet. "It shouldn't be much farther."

As Charles retrieved his satchel and his flashlight, he glanced up to see not only Penelope, Bertram, and Zed, but also two other men. They were both black, dressed in clothes from the late 1800s, and neither of them was completely there. The moonlight shone through them. One of them smiled at Charles and tipped his hat. Then they both turned around and disappeared among the trees.

Zed's heart pounded as they entered the clearing. This was the graveyard from his shared visions with Jake. There was no doubt about it. Thankfully, Jake was a hundred miles away and safe, or at least safer than he would be if he were here. As they ventured farther into the cemetery, his apprehension grew, though, wondering if he had done the right thing, if maybe Jake was needed here somehow. His thoughts were interrupted by a cry from Bertram. They had found Ephraim. He was tied to a tree, his clothes in tatters, dripping in blood.

"Dad?" Bertram ran toward the tree. "Dad, it's me."

Ephraim didn't answer.

Bertram stopped just a few feet away from him. "Dad? Oh, God."

When Zed and the others joined him, they could all see what Bertram saw. Ephraim's throat was slit open. He stared ahead with sightless eyes, an odd smile frozen on his face. The blood was already drying.

"He's gone," Bertram whispered. "We're too late."

"Did you think this was going to have a happy ending?"

The voice came from behind them. They turned around to see a man holding a knife, the blade caked in brown-red blood. A giant raven perched on his shoulder. With a flick of his wrist, all their flashlights went out, replaced by an eerie glow under their feet. The outline of the pentagram spread out across the ground, just the same as the floor of the Brown warehouse and Penelope's office, and the drawing she found among her dad's things.

"Malphas," Charles said.

"What's that?" Bertram asked.

"It's the name of the demon he's summoning. The raven is Malphas' emissary."

Bertram glanced back at the body of his father. "How bad is this demon?"

"We're fucked," Charles replied. "It won't be the end of the world tomorrow. Malphas doesn't work that way, but we're still fucked. He's a corruptor. Things will happen by increments. People will care a little less about their neighbors. It won't look bad, not at first, but eventually we won't be the good people we see ourselves as anymore. We won't be the kind-hearted heroes who stand up for what is right. We'll be the villains."

The man rolled his eyes. "A little dramatic, don't you think?"

Bertram took a step closer to Charles and the giant satchel of magical things slung over Charles' shoulder. "Is this Malphas here now?"

Charles closed his eyes. Zed had seen that expression on his face countless times, as he reached out beyond his five senses. Even Zed could feel the charge in the air, just like the moments before a thunderstorm.

"Not yet, but he's coming," Charles said when he opened his eyes again.

"Who are you?" Penelope asked the man.

He sighed. "I suppose I shouldn't be surprised your father never told you about me. He probably just wanted to forget the whole thing happened. I can't say I blame him. I'd want to forget too, but the difference between us is that he could move on with his life. I couldn't."

"Jude Hall," Bertram said.

Penelope raised an eyebrow. "Jude Hall? But you're supposed to be dead. You hanged yourself."

Jude laughed. "I *am* dead, for all intents and purposes. After tonight, though, it won't matter anymore. I'll have what want."

"Why now?" Penelope asked. "You've had forty years."

"Because I couldn't." His mouth curled up into a bitter scowl. "After what your father did to me that night, I was an invalid. I could barely move. I was bedridden for years, but then one by one, the others died, and I got better, stronger. I started making plans. I faked my death to rid myself of any obligations. On the night your father died, I knew my time had come."

Charles scanned the symbols and words arrayed around the lines of the pentagram. "You tried to summon Malphas back then, too, didn't you? Penelope's dad disrupted the spell and banished him back to the other side of the Veil, but you had to extend your own spirit out as a beacon for the demon. When everything went sideways, part of your soul must have been ripped away, and shards of it clung to everyone who was there. As the others died, those pieces came back to you."

Jude nodded. "Go on, magician, tell them the rest."

"I've studied these symbols for months, trying to pry all

their secrets out," Charles continued, "but I've come up with nothing. Now things are beginning to make sense. This pentagram is a work of genius. Evil, twisted, malevolent genius, but genius all the same. It's a circle without a beginning or an end. Recite the spell one way, and you summon a demon. Recite it another way, and you call on that demon to grant you power. That's why you killed Bobby Parker and the rest. They were sacrifices."

"And ultimately so were Roy Arnold and Patrick Wheeler, once you'd gotten them to do your dirty work for you," Zed added.

Penelope looked to Zed, a silent communication passing between them. *Keep him talking. Buy Charles time.* "What do you gain from all this?"

Zed grunted. "Same as every other jackass who tries to summon a higher-level demon. Knowledge, power, money."

"Shows how much you know. You don't understand anything." Jude jabbed the knife in his hand toward the body of Ephraim Brown still tied to the tree. "They didn't understand, either. Malphas can show those who summon him things that lie beyond the Veil, including people who have passed. If they had just let me finish, they could have talked to anyone they wanted to."

Penelope's eyes narrowed. "All this happened because you wanted to talk to someone you lost, didn't you?"

"That's not your business," Jude spat.

Penelope persisted. "Who was it?"

"You don't deserve to know."

"Then it was someone."

Jude gripped the handle of the knife tighter. "That's enough."

"It was his sister," Bertram said quietly. "She died the year before. She was only sixteen."

Jude regarded Bertram icily. "How do you know that?"

Bertram seemed equally surprised. "I … don't know."

Penelope took a step forward. "He's right, though, isn't he?"

Jude was shaking. His grief was real, and deep, and it was all he had left. He'd burn everything down before he let go of it. "So, what if he is? Malphas would have let me see her again, just one more time."

"In return for what?" Zed asked.

"What does it matter to you?" Jude worked his jaw, eyes darting from Penelope to Zed. Holding onto the demon was taking its toll. The last bit of his sanity was fraying.

"An awful lot if you're going to invite that kind of evil into the world," Zed replied.

Jude let out a humorless chuckle, and odd smile on his face. "What's a little more evil in a world like this?"

"Malphas lies," Charles said. "It's what he does."

"No, I could see her before Johnathan ruined everything, just as beautiful as the day she died." Looking at something that wasn't there, he extended his free hand up into the air. "She was reaching out a hand to me. I came so close to grasping it, and then she was ripped away from me again."

Charles shook his head. "It wasn't her. That was just a trick."

"No, it was her," Jude screamed. "I know it was her. And I'm going to see her again. Tonight."

"I wouldn't count on it." Charles pointed to Ephraim. "He gave us the key. I don't know how he did it, but before he died, he gave his son the memories of what happened here before. We know how to stop you. Like I said, this spell is a circle, with no beginning or end. Say the words in the right order and it'll send Malphas right back where he came from."

"You're bluffing."

"Try us," said Penelope.

Jude's lips pulled back in a sneer, showing his teeth. Howls rose up from the forest all around them as the shadows billowed up and daemons descended on the graveyard, but before they could attack, Zed held up the rosary Charles had given him—one of the trinkets he carried in his satchel. Zed recited the *Vade Retro Satana* just like he had before to drive the daemon away from Jake. At the same time, Penelope made a cut in the palm of her hand with Zed's pocket knife and let a trickle of blood fall on the pentagram to deflect its magic. She had to be the one, Charles said, because she carried her father's blood.

The daemons shrieked and swooped down on them, but none of them came any closer than the pentagram's perimeter. Charles began chanting, the words unfamiliar to Zed's ears, *wrong*, somehow. They physically hurt him, but he dared not stop chanting himself. Charles needed time to finish the spell.

Jude didn't seem to be bothered. "Idiots. I'll admit it, I was angry when the traps I set for each of you didn't work, maybe a little irrational even, but now I see I shouldn't have gone to the trouble."

With another flick of his wrist, Charles was lifted in the air and thrown back down to the ground. As soon as he stopped chanting the daemons doubled their screaming, and Zed couldn't hold them back any longer. The charms Charles gave him, Penelope, and Bertram meant the daemons couldn't harm any of them directly, but they could hurt in other ways.

Bertram huddled with Penelope. The shadow demons surrounded them, hissing and shrieking. As Charles tried to push himself up off the ground, they tormented him, swooping down over him until he was reduced to swatting at them, unable to get up. Zed fared a little better. They shied away from the rosary, but still they flew around him, obscuring his vision and whispering their vile lies of hopelessness and despair.

"Malphas is coming," Jude said, his voice different, not entirely his own.

He commenced his own incantation, and this time, the words tore through Zed like knives, until he could barely stand. The daemons moved in concert along the lines of the pentagram, faster and faster. The wind picked up, carrying Jude's voice up into the night sky.

Just then a figure stumbled out of the forest into the graveyard. The bottom fell out of Zed's stomach when he recognized the mop of curly brown hair.

Jake.

Zed fought through the swarm of daemons to get to him. "Jake? How did you get here?"

"I waited for Linda to fall asleep," he replied. "Then I snuck out."

"But how did you find us?" Zed's gaze went to Jake's hand clutching his side.

He had a cut over his right eye, and his clothes were torn in more than a few places.

Jake shook his head. "I don't know. Something in my head just told me the way to go."

Zed grasped him by the shoulders. "You shouldn't have come here."

"I had to, Zed. I told you. I'm supposed to be here. I ran into those shadow things in the woods. I got away from them. Mostly." Jake held up his arm. "This bracelet you gave me. It helped."

He pulled his other hand away from his side with a sticky

sucking noise. Both his hand and his shirt were covered in blood.

"Oh, my God, Jake. You're hurt."

He looked down at himself dispassionately. "Am I? I can't really feel anything."

Then his eyes rolled back into his head and he collapsed on top of Zed. Zed lowered him to the ground as gently as he could.

He took Jake's hand in his. "Hang in there. It's going to be okay."

Charles tried to stand again, but a flick of the wrist from Jude sent him flying once more. He crashed into a toppled gravestone. Jude never even broke his rhythm. Bertram and Penelope weren't faring much better among the horde of screaming shadows. Finally, a great howl rose up, one that scraped across Zed's brain. The daemons parted briefly to reveal Jude in the center of the pentagram.

"He's here," Jude said, his voice low and gravelly.

In that moment, Zed made a decision.

His abilities didn't stop at being able to sense the emotions of others. He could project them, too, make people feel things he wanted them to feel. Usually he pushed positive emotions—hope, confidence, contentment—and even then, never too much, just enough to give others whatever they needed to work through the problems in their lives. That's what he'd done with Annie, but he could make people feel other emotions, too. That day he focused all he had at Jude. One word passed his lips.

Fear.

Penelope couldn't see through the thick, black cloud of screaming daemons. She and Bertram were separated from

Charles and Zed. Between the daemons' shrieking and Jude's chanted words echoing in her head, she could hardly even think. When the daemons had come, Bertram took her by the arm and pulled her behind a gravestone, though it proved to be an imperfect shelter. Bertram shielded them both as best he could. Charles' bracelets kept the daemons from hurting them, but there were so many. Penelope didn't know if their magic would withstand the barrage. And if Jude succeeded in calling Malphas, it wouldn't matter anyway.

Through the swirl of daemons, she caught a glimpse of Zed ... and someone else. The newcomer said something to Zed, and then the man collapsed. Zed knelt over him, grabbing his hand.

A cry loud enough to shake the gravestone she and Bertram hid behind reverberated through the cemetery, and the daemons stopped. Jude stood in the middle of the pentagram, or so Penelope thought until she realized his feet weren't touching the ground. Though the air had stilled, his clothes and his hair still moved as if blown by the wind.

"He's here." Jude's lips moved, but the voice didn't belong to him.

Zed glared at him, an expression on his face Penelope had never seen before, and one she hoped to never see again. For the first time since she'd known him, she was afraid of him.

Jude wavered as the emotion overtook him. He clutched the sides of his head and screamed. The giant raven on his shoulder took flight, and with it, the daemons rose into the sky. Jude staggered a few feet, swiping at imagined foes, until he collapsed to the ground, curled into a ball, with his hands over his head.

"Keep chanting, Charles," Zed yelled.

Charles, still gathering his wits after the abrupt end to his second flight through the air, began his spell again. This time, Jude, crazed with fear, couldn't stop him from banishing Malphas back to the other side of the Veil. The daemons' shrieks and the call of the raven faded away until Charles' words were all that was left. When he stopped speaking, the woods were absolutely still and quiet, as if the whole world had just paused.

It didn't last.

Jude screamed, a wail of pure anguish and rage. The emotion knocked Zed to the ground. He almost blacked out from the intensity of it, but then Jude's cry was cut off abruptly. The magician collapsed, the handle of the pocket knife Penelope had used to cut herself sticking out from the back of his neck.

The two ghosts appeared to Charles again at the edge of the graveyard. The one who had tipped his hat before did so again. This time he spoke, and though he made no sound, Charles had no trouble understanding the words he mouthed.

"We'll be seeing you again, soon, Mr. Delacorte."

5.

Monday, October 30, 1972

PENELOPE SET THE ROCK PAPERWEIGHT back down on her desk and stared at it. She'd taken the stone with her to Happiness, hoping, maybe stupidly, that somehow her father would be there with her. She still wasn't ready to let him go.

He was there in a way, she supposed, smiling sadly. The time he'd spent teaching her how to properly throw a knife hadn't gone to waste, though she still didn't quite understand what happened when Jude lost control. Zed had … done something to him, that she was sure of. He was vague about it afterward, his focus more on getting his friend help.

Zed said his name was Jake. He confessed to her the truth about their relationship while she waited with him in the emergency room of the hospital for word about Jake's injuries. The two of them were the only ones awake. Bertram and Charles had both long since fallen asleep.

She asked him why he hadn't told her sooner. He said he was afraid of how she'd react. She'd grasped his hand and told him he was her friend, and she just wanted him to be happy. After everything they'd been through together, she couldn't really say much else.

A knock at the door brought her back to the present. She found Bertram on her porch.

"I can't stay long," he said as he stepped inside. "I just stopped by to say good-bye."

She nodded. "I figured this was coming. Where are you headed? Back to Atlanta?"

Bertram shook his head. "Virginia. I need to spend a little time with my mom. I owe it to her after everything she's been through. Things are going to be tough for a little while. It's going to take some time to wind down the business. And then there's the other stuff that needs taking care of. There are a lot of things my family's done, a lot of dark secrets that need to be brought into the light of day. I just need a little time to sort through what's in my head."

They had buried Ephraim in Happiness. They'd never be able to explain his death to anyone without raising questions none of them were prepared to answer. As far as anyone else was concerned, Ephraim Brown would forever be just another missing person.

The package arrived for Penelope the day after their return from Happiness—Ephraim's magic book, and a letter, explaining what he had done. He knew there was a chance he might die sooner rather than later, and so he bought himself a little insurance by casting the spell they'd discovered the remnants of. It was supposed to transfer his memories of the ritual in college to Bertram if and when he passed on. Those memories helped them defeat Jude Hall, but, as often happened with magic, the effects spilled over. Bertram found himself in possession of a little more knowledge than he necessarily knew how to handle.

As for the book itself, it was a lot more than the simple

recipe book Ephraim led Penelope to believe. Many of the spells dated to before the Civil War, and some were even older, going all the way back to the Brown's ancestors in Wales.

Despite the general pain in the ass Bertram could be, Penelope had to admit she hated to see him leave. "You'll come back to visit?"

He leaned over and kissed her on the cheek. "I'll be back. I promise you. You're not getting rid of me that easily, Dreadful Penny."

Zed was working near the front of the bookstore when the bell jingled and Jake entered, still limping, still with a bandage above his right eye.

Zed smiled. "Hi, there."

Jake smiled back. "Hi."

Zed pointed to the bandage. "How are you feeling?"

"Like I got mauled by a horde of shadow demons," Jake replied, "but well enough to at least leave the house."

"I hope I didn't cause you too much trouble with Linda."

Jake chuckled. "Are you kidding? She wants to know who my dealer is."

Zed had stayed away to avoid any more questions about their relationship, but it hadn't been easy. Not a minute passed that he didn't fight the urge to check in on Jake.

Even at that moment Zed just wanted to throw his arms around him. "I'm really glad you're doing better."

Jake peered over Zed's shoulder. "Is ... ah ... Mr. Keller here?"

"He had to step out for an hour or so. We can talk."

"Look, I—"

Zed held up a hand. "You know, I understand if you want

to call things off. You didn't sign up for this. I mean, evil magicians calling forth Dukes of Hell from the netherworld isn't usually what we deal with, but I can't say it's the first time we've had a run-in with the things that go bump in the night. And I can't ask you to stay for that."

Jake stood silent for a moment. "Do you want me to stay?"

"What?"

"Do you want me to stay?" Jake repeated.

"Of course," Zed replied.

"Then I want to stay."

Zed sighed. "Jake—"

This time Jake held up a hand. "No, you don't get to unilaterally make decisions. We share something special, and I'm not ready to let that go."

Zed started to say something else, but then the door opened, and a slight, bald man wearing a pair of round glasses entered the store.

Zed nodded at him. "Mr. Keller."

He barely acknowledged Zed as he strode to the back of the store.

"We close at six today," Zed said to Jake.

Jake grinned. "I'll be here at six-thirty."

Charles held the book up to the light. When he found it, the leather had been worn off the corners of the cover, exposing the crumbling boards underneath. The spine was cocked and frayed. Some of the signatures were loose, and a lot of the pages showed signs of foxing.

But now it was perfect.

The new leather cover glistened and the gold leaf gleamed. This was Millie's book. Making it beautiful was the least he could do for her. He hadn't seen Millie since coming back from Happiness, nor had he traveled to her version of Harlem again. Isaiah Jenkins' memories were fading away bit by bit, everything except Millie's voice and the sight of her in her blue sequined dress. He didn't know if what he had encountered was really her ghost or just an elaborate illusion. In one sense, it didn't really matter.

Charles put the book down and turned his attention to one that still needed a lot of work. He carried it to his work table, but before he sat down, he turned on the radio. An old spiritual, "Mary Don't You Weep," poured out. Charles picked up his X-acto knife and began to cut away the book's old cover.

Penelope was headed upstairs to her apartment when someone else knocked on the door. This time, Dan waited for her on the front porch.

"Dan? Hi. Come in," she said. "What can I do for you?"

He seemed anxious. He didn't know exactly what to do with his hands, putting them first in his pockets, then by his sides, and finally behind his back. "Well, truth be told, I was a little worried about you. You didn't show up at the shop on Thursday. Is everything okay?"

Penelope suddenly felt sick. Thursday. They were supposed to have dinner. "Oh, God, Dan. I'm so sorry. I had a case blow up and wound up having to go out of town."

He raised an eyebrow. "Nothing too serious I hope."

By "serious" he clearly meant "dangerous."

Penelope dodged the question. "It's … been taken care of."

"Good. I'm glad to hear it. And I understand. I know being a detective isn't exactly a nine-to-five job." He paused, still obviously nervous. "So, I was wondering if I could also ask you a favor."

"Sure. What is it?"

"Do you think you could have your friend bring by her locket, the one you showed me before?"

"I think so." Penelope didn't tell him she still had the heart-shaped locket from Carolyn's secret admirer in an envelope in her desk.

"Great," Dan said. "I actually got in some pieces by the same silversmith, and I'd like to compare them to see if I can narrow down the year they were made."

"I'll talk to her tomorrow. Maybe I can bring the locket by the shop myself."

Dan managed a smile. "Yeah, I'd like that. I mean, if it's not too much trouble."

An awkward silence settled between them. Dan didn't make a move to leave, and Penelope didn't necessarily want him to go, though she wasn't sure what else to say, other than to apologize again. "Look, I'm really sorry about blowing you off. Is there any way I can make it up?"

He shrugged. "Why don't you have dinner with me tonight?"

Penelope glanced upstairs. She wasn't really looking forward to the TV dinner waiting for her in the freezer, and after everything that had happened, Dan's company sounded awfully appealing. "Sure. Just let me get a jacket."

As she passed by the door to the office, her gaze went to her desk. Her paperweight wasn't where she'd left it.

ABOUT THE AUTHOR

J. Matthew Saunders, a native of Greenville, South Carolina, is the author of the *Daughters of Shadow and Blood* trilogy about the Brides of Dracula as well as numerous published fantasy and horror short stories. He received a B.A. in history from Vanderbilt University and a master's degree from the School of Journalism at the University of South Carolina. He received his law degree in California and practiced there as an attorney for several years.

He is an unapologetic European history geek, enjoys the Celtic fiddle, and makes a mean sun-dried tomato-basil pesto. He currently lives near Charlotte, North Carolina with his wife and two children. To find out more, visit www.jmsaunders.com.